DIABLERIE

DIABLERIE

A NOVEL

WALTER MOSLEY

BLOOMSBURY

Published by Bloomsbury USA, New York
Distributed to the trade by Macmillan

All papers used by Bloomsbury USA are natural, recyclable products made from wood grown in well-managed forests. The manufacturing processes conform to the environmental regulations of the country of origin.

LIBRARY OF CONGRESS CATALOGING-IN-PUBLICATION DATA

Mosley, Walter.
Diablerie : a novel / Walter Mosley.—1st U.S. ed.
p. cm.
ISBN-13: 978-1-59691-397-4 (alk. paper)
ISBN-10: 1-59691-397-5 (alk. paper)
1. Memory—Fiction. 2. Self-perception—Fiction. I. Title.
PS3563.O88456D53 2008
813'.54—dc22
2007018826

First U.S. Edition 2008

1 3 5 7 9 10 8 6 4 2

Typeset by Hewer Text UK Ltd, Edinburgh
Printed in the United States of America by Quebecor World Fairfield

The apartment reeked from the acrid odor of roaches—a whole colony, tens of thousands of them, seething and unseen in the walls and under the dull, splintery floorboards of the vacant tenement apartment.

"Isn't it great, Daddy?" Seela said.

Her smile was exultant. She hugged my arm.

I turned my head toward the window looking out on the East Village street. There I saw a Rastafarian wearing clothes that were once bright but now had faded into dull tatters, two transvestite prostitutes, and a powerful-looking drunk who was having a loud disagreement with a newspaper vending machine.

"It's only twenty-two hundred and Millie's going to split it with me," Seela was saying. "We can move in tomorrow."

"It looks like a dicey neighborhood, honey," I said, unable to keep the whine out of my voice. "What if that guy down there goes crazy and pushes his way in here?"

"Oh, Dad. Lots of kids from NYU live around here."

"What's so bad about the dorms?"

"I hate the dorms. There's always noise and parties and drama like you wouldn't believe. Please."

I'd never thought that my daughter was beautiful; she wasn't even pretty. But Seela was young and slender, and she had a friendly smile. While she beamed at me, the feeling that lurked in

1

my shoulder blades took over. Not an emotion or something physical like pain or heat or cold, it was more akin to a void, a sensual numbness. I wanted to say something, to tell her that she deserved better, but the words didn't come and even the ideas behind them fell away. I couldn't speak, couldn't feel for her safety.

She stood there smiling at me, believing that I was her loving, concerned father.

Seela was medium brown, halfway between my dark color and her mother's light, coppery hue. Those big eyes stared into mine and I looked around the apartment, pretending to be assessing its worth.

"Can I have the money, Dad?" she asked. "It's not that much more than the dorms and, and I could get a part-time job."

"Sure. I guess. But you're the one who has to convince your mother if she starts to go crazy. I just took my Sunday afternoon to see this place, but if your mom goes nuts about the neighborhood, well . . ." I let the words hang in the air.

"She'll listen to you," my daughter said confidently.

Seela threw her arms around my neck and kissed me on the cheek. She might as well have kissed the wall or that drunk in the street. It wasn't that I felt nothing—not exactly. The truth was I couldn't feel anything but dread of those roaches teeming, unseen but still there.

"Your mom went to the hairdressers," I said. "She's waiting for me on Fourteenth. You want to have dinner with us?"

"No thanks. I'm seeing Jamal and his friends for dinner, then we're going to this indie film called *Herd*. It's all about . . ."

While she talked I shifted my gaze back to the window, this time into an apartment across the way. A couple was standing there arguing. The woman gesticulated with her hands above her head, held like claws, while he had loose fists up at chest level like a boxer reflexively defending himself, looking for an opening.

"I've got to get out of here," I said, not necessarily to Seela.

"Daddy, I was telling you about *Herd*."

"I'll call you at the dorms tomorrow. Talk to you then, honey."

I was on the street before I realized that I hadn't kissed her good-bye.

I never liked kissing all that much—didn't see what people got out of it, really. Mona complained that I wasn't romantic enough when we made love. She pulled away emotionally but I wasn't terribly bothered. I sometimes grumbled when we hadn't had sex in more than two weeks. But then I started seeing Svetlana two or three days a week and things were better, at least for me, at least when I was sitting there quietly in Svetlana's West Side studio, after having made love, with the sun shining in and her reading Russian newspapers and smoking European cigarettes. It felt like I was safe then. I seemed always to be looking for a cubbyhole or corner to sit in, a place I could be quiet and unnoticed.

All I had to do was pay the rent and keep a tab open at the supermarket in Svetlana's name and she was mine. There was never any evidence of any other man in the house. When I called, she usually made time to talk, even if there was an exam coming up or she had a paper due.

She said she liked me because I didn't abuse her. She never worried about me hitting her. When her mother was dying, I bought her round-trip tickets and gave her enough money to keep afloat in Kiev for a month. After she came back, I told Mona I was going to a convention in Atlantic City so that I could spend two days at Svetlana's. I thought that she'd want to talk, but she didn't. We made love, had sex, once every four waking hours for two days and then she got restless—or maybe it just seemed that way to me.

She'd pick up a paper and then put it down, light a cigarette and put it out almost immediately, then go to the window, searching Eighth Avenue with her brooding gaze.

"Do you need me to leave, Lana?" I asked her.

"No," she said, shaking her tousled blonde hair. "Why?"

Svetlana was twenty-one, already in graduate school studying international relations at CUNY. Her figure was slight, almost boyish. Her hands were powerful though. She could hurt me with her grip. I liked that. Sometimes, when we were having sex and I couldn't come to orgasm, Lana would grab the back of my neck with her left hand and squeeze until the pain went down into my shoulders. While she did this, she'd smile like a naughty child doing something that she was bound to get away with. Whenever she did this, I had intense orgasms, like none that I remembered. Once I even passed out, something I hadn't done since my drinking days in the late seventies and before.

Sometimes I'd tell Lana, "Squeeze my neck, baby," but she wouldn't obey.

"It has to be my choice when," she'd tell me. "Otherwise it wouldn't work anymore."

I knew that she was very smart, that she would move on once she had her degree and started working in international finance or diplomacy. But I didn't care.

I didn't care about much. This lack of sentiment didn't bother me unless Mona or Seela would complain. But then the void in the hollow of my shoulders would take over and I'd watch an old movie or go see Svetlana. Sometimes I'd just go to work or to bed—it was all the same to me. I was lucky in that way.

Mona had a favorite coffee shop on Fourteenth Street near Fifth Avenue. She usually went there on Fridays. "To decompress after a week of bullshit," she'd say. It was called Augie's and they made a French roast coffee so strong that I had to cut it with an equal portion of steamed milk. But Mona loved the bitter brew and the tough Irish waitresses, two of whom had worked there since Mona was a teenager.

That Sunday she was sitting at the counter holding her long fingers to her lips in a smoker's pose. Mona hadn't had a cigarette in twenty-five years, since before I met her, but she still held her hands like a smoker.

She'd let her hair go gray, but for some reason, with the help of the bright carmine lipstick she wore, this only served to make her look younger. She was in much better shape than I was; an hour and a half in the gym six days a week made her muscles feel like tough young bamboo: resistant and resilient, springy with hardly a trace of softness.

That day she wore the maroon dress suit with red high heels and a scarlet bag.

The lady in red, I thought.

"How was it?" Mona asked as I came up to the stool next to her.

It was decided, long before, that I would talk to Seela when she asked for something big. I didn't mind saying no and I never got upset.

"Fine. Clean. Sixth-floor walk-up. If nothing else, she'll get a little exercise."

I sat down. Mona took the imaginary cigarette from her lips, her island-brown eyes studying me.

"What?" I asked after an appropriate wait.

"Why do you stay with me, Benny?"

"Come again?" I said, to keep my distance until I could gauge the virulence of her attack.

Because it would certainly be an attack. Mona wanted more out of me, more out of everything. Seela wasn't a good-enough student, I wasn't a good-enough husband, her parents had never done right by her either. Only her cousin Minna, who'd died of cancer years ago, had ever been exactly what Mona wanted.

"Are you . . . happy?" she asked.

"Of course I am," I said. "I could be dead but instead I have a daughter at university and a wife so pretty that she could have a twenty-year-old boyfriend if she wanted."

"Bullshit."

"What's wrong, Mona?"

"I think it's because it would cost you too much," she speculated. "College plus two households. You'd have to take care of me for life, you know."

"I see you've thought about it," I said, still feinting, still gauging the opposition.

"Do you love me?" She brought the phantom cigarette halfway to her mouth.

"Yes. But it's more than that, you know."

"No, I don't know."

"Do you remember when we met?" I asked.

"Yeah?"

"I was sick and getting sicker all the time."

"You had viral pneumonia," she said, as if correcting me. "You needed rest and medicine."

6

"That was the outside of it. But on the inside I felt that I was hanging over a precipice, like I was dangling from a frayed rope that was only holding on by a thread."

"You were sick," she said. "People feel like that when they're sick."

"No. I was like that all the time. I'd left Boulder and stopped drinking. Every day I felt like I was going to fall into that hole. The pneumonia was just a part of it. I ate junk food and was depressed but didn't know it. When you nursed me to health, you saved me from falling in. You do it all the time, almost every day. That, that hole, that abyss, is a fixture in my mind, and if it weren't for you, I'd have fallen in and broken my neck a long time ago."

I don't know why I said all that to Mona right then. I hadn't even seen Barbara Knowland yet. I hadn't thought about Colorado in many years.

"What are you saying, Benny?" Mona asked. "Is this some movie you saw or something?"

"What do you mean?"

"Abyss? Frayed rope? Holding on by a thread?"

"It might be trite but I feel it all the time," I said, lying by telling the truth. "I felt it today with Seela. If I didn't have a family, I wouldn't have anything."

There was a colony of competing and conflicting thoughts behind Mona's stern grimace, like the roaches I smelled teeming beneath Seela's floors.

My words stymied the argument she was nursing. They rang of truth somewhere, and Mona always reacted to truth. She was angry that she couldn't let the rage in her breast roil up against me. I had admitted something personal and she had no rebuttal against that.

7

"But you don't tell us that," Mona said. "You just, you just sit there staring out the window."

"Yeah, I know. Way in the back of my head there's this, there's this, I don't know. You're the only one who sees it, honey. When you call me on it, you call me back."

"You still don't talk to me."

"What am I doing right now?"

The frustration showed in Mona's slender, still quite lovely face. The only thing I had to do was to stifle the grin rising from my diaphragm. Whenever I defeated her in our jousts of words, I wanted to smirk—not laugh or smile or chuckle. I wanted to gloat over her stumble. Here she had laid a trap for me, the goal of which neither of us knew or understood. We just wrangled, disputed over anything: Seela's future, our sex routines, what life had or had not brought to either of us.

"You're saying that I save you?" she asked. "Me. The woman you barely touch, hardly ever talk to. Me, the one lying in your bed when you come back from who knows where in the middle of the night."

~

Three months before, the phone rang at a little after two in the morning. Mona answered it.

"Benny?" she said, tugging my shoulder. "It's work."

"Hello?" I called into the void of the receiver, wondering what reason anyone at work had to call me in the middle of the night.

"I want to suck your cock right now," Svetlana whispered into my ear. "I got up thinking about you and now my pussy needs your cock."

"So . . . what's wrong?" I asked, trying to keep my erection down and Mona from figuring out it wasn't work at all.

"If you don't come fuck me right now, I'm going back to my old boyfriend in Coney Island. My pussy is crying over you, weeping all over my bed."

"Did you try the JCL?"

"I've got to have your cock right now, before one hour I have to have your cock deep, deep, deep."

"Okay. All right. I'll come in. Yeah. Run the other jobs, all except the totals routine. If you run that, the whole system will go down."

I stumbled from the bed gasping for breath, my nearly fifty-year-old cock stiff as a mummy's thumb. I was thankful that Mona didn't turn on the light, just yakked at me in the dark room.

"Who was it?"

"I don't know who's on night shift anymore," I said. "But the checking account subroutine went down and I have to go fix it. Fix it."

I had hurried on my pants and was buttoning a loose-fitting shirt that hung down over any vestiges of the erection.

I put on shoes with no socks and then hit my shins on the night table.

"You haven't had to go in at night in twelve years," Mona said, doing the math in her head and sounding suspicious.

She turned on the light.

At this time of morning she looked all of her forty-five years, and then some. Sleep was hard on Mona. Her disappointments and perceived failures gathered in the pool of night.

"I don't know what it is. Maybe some date trigger or an update to the system that no longer accepts the JCL."

"You know I don't understand anything about computers," she said angrily.

"I don't know why," I said in retort. "I've been a programmer ever since we met. I talk about it every goddamned day."

"Don't raise your voice to me."

"And you could get your fuck ass outta bed and offer to help me, to make me a coffee or call me a car. Instead you complain that you don't know what I'm talking about when I'm going to work to pay the rent."

"You know I hate it when you use that kind of language."

"And you know I have to go to work."

On the street, in the nighttime East Side, there was a solitary yellow cab prowling for a fare. I waved it down and hopped in. It smelled of woody incense and resounded with Indian music. The driver sang along with the high-pitched woman vocalist. He only asked me for my destination. I only gave him Svetlana's address.

She was waiting at the door in a bright yellow terry cloth robe.

"Take off your clothes and lie down on the couch," she commanded.

I was very excited, still erect. I did what she said in seconds. She dropped her robe, squatted down over me.

"Is your heart beating hard?" she asked.

I nodded, suddenly aware of the thunder in my chest.

"I don't want you to move," she said. "I will do everything. Just lie there and feel it. If you move, I will scratch your face with my nails and you will have to explain that to your wife. Do you understand?"

I nodded again, my heart doubling its effort.

As Lana lowered down onto me, bringing me inside her, she asked, "Was that your wife who answered the phone?"

I cried out a syllable that has no counterpart in English and nodded.

She was rocking back and forth slowly.

"Was she suspicious?"

"Yes."

"Will she leave you?"

"Only, only a little wary," I said. "She thinks I'm at work."

"Do you want me to make her leave you?"

"Do you want me?" I asked, more timidly than I would have liked.

"No."

"Then why . . . ?"

Svetlana, her elbows on her knees, started moving her hips in a slow circle. The sensation took away my breath.

"Look at me," she said. "In my eyes."

I gazed at her gray eyes, eyes that saw me but seemed as if they were on some other plane. They were hungry eyes, wolflike.

"Talk to me," she said. "No. Don't look away. Look at me and talk to me while I fuck you."

"What should I say?"

She said something that I didn't understand.

That's when the void began to creep out from its lair. I could feel it extending from the caves in my shoulders where it slumbered. I moved my head to the left, trying to avoid the cold grip of deadness. I closed my eyes and Svetlana slapped me—hard. It hurt and in the pain I could see something . . .

It wasn't anything I remembered at all, just a shadow that I knew hid an entire mountain. For some reason this terrified me.

11

When I opened my eyes, I was standing over Svetlana. The coffee table was upended and she was on the floor. Obviously I had dropped her there.

I was shivering, holding my hands like the woman I saw across the street from Seela's new apartment. Svetlana was frozen between fear of me and fear for me; I saw this in her face.

I didn't know what to do so I grabbed my pants from the floor and put them on. Svetlana had just said something but again I didn't understand. We stared at each other over the void of physical violence, both of us silenced and fearful.

The phone rang then. It was a loud, brash ring, like old phones made when I was a child. It seemed that the ring was something calling to me from a long time ago: my dead father with one last admonition, an appointment I had failed to keep . . .

The phone had rung six or seven times when I realized that Svetlana wasn't answering it, maybe she didn't even hear it. She was mesmerized by me. The look of fear and wonder in her face was in turn fascinating; it seemed to have something to do with that ring.

"Lana, the phone. Lana!"

Now aware of the ringing, she crawled toward the phone, which was on the floor, and answered: "Hello? . . . Yes, Mrs. Hightower . . . No . . . My boyfriend was playing around and he fell . . . No, nobody is hurt. I'm so sorry we disturbed you . . . I know it is late . . . Bye. Sorry."

When she hung up, I said, "I have to go."

Svetlana got to her feet and touched my left hand. I could feel it distinctly. It was a light touch, almost a tickle. I turned away and went out her door.

12

On the street I realized that I was still shivering. I was trying to remember what we were talking about before I dropped her. I stood there for many minutes but the conversation was gone.

~

"If I'm such a savior," Mona said to me at the counter at Augie's three months later, "then come with me to the banquet tonight."

I hated Mona's work functions. She was a magazine editor, freelance. She worked for quasi-intellectual fashion magazines. Her friends were the gushing emotional sorts or aloof scholarly types who asked questions that I didn't even understand.

"So you save me just to punish me?" I joked, hoping that she only wanted to see me squirm.

"Really, Benny. Rudy bagged out and I can't go alone. You know, some people have started saying that I really don't have a husband at all, that I made you up because I'm a lesbian and I don't want anybody to know it."

"They'd like your fantasy girlfriend more than they'll like me."

"I saved your life," she said inflecting her words with false drama. "Now it's your turn."

We took a taxi to our place on Fifty-first near the East River. It was a nice-size, prewar apartment, with thirteen-foot ceilings and more than enough room for a one-child family. We had a big window that looked out over the water into Queens. Sometimes I'd sit in the white stuffed chair and watch the river for hours.

It was easy for me to lose track of time, which is why I adhered to such a rigid daily schedule. I left the house for work every day at 8:25, getting to the main offices of Our Bank at Forty-second and

Madison by 8:50. I left work when the job was done and came right home. Schedules kept my mind, and me, from wandering. Left with no destination or time limit, I could walk all day or sit in a coffee shop until it closed for the night.

"Are you wearing that?" Mona asked me.

I had been standing at the picture window, looking at the skies fading over Queens, holding my hand up to the pane as if I were gauging the city's anatomical form.

"What's wrong with what I'm wearing?" I asked.

I had on a tan jacket, dark brown pants and shoes, and a light-yellow shirt.

"Not the bow tie, Benny."

"When did you stop calling me 'honey'?"

Mona had donned a very dark, thin-strapped gray dress that made her body look no more than thirty. Her deep brown eyes shone and her silvery, straightened mane was tied up at the back of her head like the comb of some exotic rain forest bird.

"The first year that you forgot my birthday," she said.

The simplicity and quickness of her reply shocked me. When was her birthday? February? And how many years had it been since I remembered?

"I don't have any regular ties," I said.

"So don't wear one. Go loose for a change."

The Houghton Arms was one of the oldest hotels in the city. It was on Park, above Forty-sixth and below Fiftieth, but I never remembered the exact cross-street. Mona and I decided to walk since the weather was fair and to clear the air between us.

I was quiet on the way because nothing I could say would make up for the years of forgotten birthdays. I was disquieted also because of my abandonment of our daughter and my ever-increasing distance from everyone, including my illicit lover, and because I didn't care at all about Mona's unheralded birthdays. What difference did any of it make? Why were we even walking together?

"Benny?"

"Uh-huh."

"Have you thought about going back into therapy?"

"Say what?"

"You heard me." We'd come to a stop at a light, at Fiftieth and Park.

~

There was a brief span of time, four years earlier, when I'd wake up yelling every night. This had gone on for three months when Mona finally said that either I went into therapy or I slept in another room.

She found me the therapist, Dr. Adrian Shriver, and I reluctantly made an appointment. The nightmares stopped a week before the first session. But I went anyway; Mona insisted.

The truth was, I would have been happy to sleep in a separate room. After all, we rarely had sex and never held each other in the night, we didn't confide little secrets about our days. And though she didn't snore, Mona breathed heavily—sometimes I felt that she was sucking all the oxygen out of the room.

But I couldn't move to another bed. Mona would have seen that as a betrayal—even if she was the one who demanded it.

Eventually I told Mona that I had quit therapy. In reality Dr. Shriver had let me go.

15

"It has been three years," he said to me one autumnal day, "and you haven't told me anything substantive about your family history or your childhood."

"Is that important?" I asked him.

"Let's take a break for a while, Mr. Dibbuk," Dr. Shriver said. "The dreams haven't returned. Maybe you can come back when you feel safe enough to reveal yourself."

～

"Back to therapy," I said. "Why should I? I haven't had one of those dreams in years. I'm fine. I'm happy."

"Like hell you are. Anytime I ever come up on you when you're alone, you have the saddest look on your face."

The light changed to green but I turned to Mona instead of crossing. There was serious concern in her face for me. I wondered what it might be like to feel that way: pained at someone else's grief, a grief that person didn't even know.

"I'm fine," I said, and we crossed together. "What's the dinner for tonight?"

Sighing in defeat she said, "It's the premiere issue of a new magazine I'm working for—*Diablerie*."

"What's that mean?"

"It depends," Mona said. The strain in her voice lightened as she began to talk about her work. "The word can mean either mischievous or evil. The magazine is a blend of both—articles about sexy new stars, naughty getaways, and puff pieces about people in the news. Tonight they're going to have Barbara Knowland as a guest at one of the tables. She may even address the audience."

"Who's Barbara Knowland?" I asked, happy not to be discussing my lapsed therapy.

"She was the woman who was held hostage by that guy who went on that killing rampage in Tennessee and Arkansas," Mona said. "The one the police held for a year and a half because they thought that she was involved with the killings."

"Yeah," I said, "I remember. They finally found those videotapes of her tied up and that guy, whatshisname, came out of the coma . . ."

"Ron Tellman," Mona said. "He testified that Cargill, the killer, kept the Knowland woman gagged and handcuffed to a steel bolt in the back of his covered pickup truck."

"Damn. So now she's written a memoir or something?"

"*Scorched Earth: From Communes to Killers*, by Barbara Knowland."

We were at the hotel by then. We signed in at the reception table and got our name tags: MONA VALERIA and MONA VALERIA'S GUEST. I went to the table in the main hall while Mona made the rounds, chatting up friends, potential clients, and competitors at the cocktail party held in the lobby.

There were forty-six round tables set up for the banquet. All the chairs were empty. Only the black-clad waitstaff was there, bustling around putting salads at place settings and making sure everything was perfect.

"Wine, sir?"

I looked up to see a very lovely young Asian woman carrying a bottle of red wine in one hand and white in the other. She was quite fetching in her short black skirt and black stockings that let through the barest glimmer of pale skin.

I almost said yes. My incipient reply was so obvious that the question of which kind rose almost visibly in her throat.

"No," I said. "I better not."

"Why not? It's a party, right?" Asian features with a New York soul.

"I took a drink one time when I was on Sunset Boulevard in Los Angeles," I said. "The next thing I knew, I was waking up in a flophouse on the Bowery . . . five and a half years later."

"That's not good."

I could have been friends with that woman. I was sure of it.

"You have Diet Coke?"

"Cola," she said, annunciating the syllables.

"Okay. Cola," I replied, mimicking her locution.

She smiled for me and went away. I decided that it was worth coming to the party after all. Those few words with that lovely child more than made up for the blowhards, backstabbers, and twits that inhabited Mona's life.

I was watching the waitress walk across the large hall when a woman said, "Ben?"

There was a hand on my shoulder. She was fortysomething, five foot two, natural brown hair with only a strand or two of gray. She wore a low-cut blue dress that seemed to be a size too small and had a shawl made from peacock feathers pinned to her left shoulder.

Her eyes were different colors, brown and green. For some reason this was very important to me. It meant something.

"Ben?"

"Yes?" I said, telling her with the tone of that single-syllable utterance that I didn't know her.

"It's me," she said. "Star."

"Um . . . I seem to have forgotten . . ."

" 'I seem to have forgotten'?" she said, as if those words shouldn't have come from me. "Come on, Ben. You can't forget me, us, that day . . . not something like that."

18

She didn't have a name tag identifying her field or magazine. "What day was that?" I asked.

"Pretending won't wash it away, Ben. We were both there."

"I have no idea what you're talking about, Star."

"June 28, 1979," she said, more an accusation than information.

"That's back when I was still drinking," I said. "I was just telling the waitress there that I've forgotten more nights than I remember from those days."

"Forgotten? You don't . . . ?" Star's face twisted into an expression that was either fear or distaste—maybe both. "Why would you come here if you don't remember?"

"Listen, lady, I don't know what you're talking about. I'm here with my wife because she's an editor for the magazine. That's all. I don't know you. I don't remember you. Maybe we met a long time ago when I was drunk. If we did, I hope I was a gentleman. If I wasn't, I hope you got over it."

Suspicion overwhelmed any other emotion in Star's reaction to me.

"Here's your diet cola, sir," the young Asian waitress said.

I was happy for the interruption.

"Thank you," I said, and when I turned back, Star was gone.

"This is my husband, Benny Dibbuk," Mona was saying.

The table was full now, as was the rest of the hall. My wife was introducing me to Harvard Rollins, some sort of fact-checker for the magazine.

"Ben," I said, a little too forcefully, "Ben Dibbuk. So you're an editor too, Mr. Rollins?"

"No. Not me. I wouldn't know what to do with a comma to save my life."

"We do more than add commas," Mona said, putting her hand on the handsome white man's forearm.

Everyone at the table seemed to think that this was a hilarious joke.

"So what do you do?" I asked as a kind of shelter against the laughter I couldn't share in.

"Kinda like a detective. Sorta like that. When they get a story in that no one else has, they put me on the trail to make sure everything's copacetic, if you know what I mean. Mostly it's on the phone, and Internet stuff, but I hit the bricks now and then."

Harvard was lean and olive-skinned, in his midthirties. His eyes wanted to be brown but didn't quite make it. His mustache had to have been waxed to stay so perfect.

"Wow. Is that common? Having a detective on staff?"

"I'm not a licensed P.I.," he said, "just an ex-cop who doesn't want the NYPD to send him into back-alley crack dens anymore."

Mona loved it. One of the things that she'd always felt had been kept from her was excitement. The reason she was attracted to me in the first place was because I had hitchhiked around the country, been a hobo, a drunk, and a womanizer—that was until I got a job programming computers and started living like a regular guy.

"What about you, Ben?" Harvard asked me.

"Do you ever sit at your desk copying notes from a piece of paper onto a computer?" I asked him.

"Sometimes. I transcribe tapes, copy notes from interviews."

"Okay," I said. "Now imagine doing it with numbers, and not all the numbers, just the ones and the zeros."

"Yeah?"

"That's what I've done every day for more than twenty years."

At other tables people were laughing and joking around, but in our little corner there was a solid five seconds of blank silence. No one knew what to say about the tedium of my life. Everyone, I was sure, felt sorry for me—everyone except Mona, who, I hoped, would never bring me to another work-related event.

She glared at me and I pretended not to notice.

After that the conversation broke down and people turned to whomever it was they sat next to. I was placed beside a young woman named Daria Hunt, who edited a section of the magazine called Toys.

"What's that?" I asked, as I was supposed to do.

"The magazine is for twenty- to thirtysomethings, mostly white," the tiny, pale-skinned woman said, "upwardly mobile, urban, conservatives-thinking-they're-liberal, prescription-drug dependent or alcoholic, college-educated, postfeminist, post-Christian office workers. Maybe Wall Street, maybe Fifth Avenue. And what, you ask, would this surprisingly large group of people want to know more than anything?"

I was completely entranced, forgetting the handsome but humble ex-cop and the mysterious, mistaken Star. Daria Hunt filled up my horizon with her sharp wit and extraordinarily accurate sound bites.

"I have no idea," I said slowly, the counterpoint to her fast tongue.

"Toys," the plain Jane with the bedroom eyes said.

"Like Legos?"

"Maybe. Yeah, Legos for the thirty-year-old, latent-adolescent stockbroker who both lives and works on Maiden Lane. He also needs a sixty-inch plasma TV, a radio-controlled multicolored lamp that goes from green to red depending on how the stock

21

market is doing at any given moment, and a handheld, twelve-ounce computer that could land a rover on Jupiter while downloading gobs of porn featuring women who only look like children and men he really wants for himself."

"I see," I said. "And what do the women in this select group want?"

"Sex," Daria said, throwing up her hands. "Sex stories, sex toys, sexy underwear, sex inhibitors, sex stimulants. Sex aroma therapy, orgasm gauges, dental dams, female condoms, and let's not forget video phones for a secret worldwide link where they can anonymously expose themselves to men anywhere, at any time, while never having to smell their panting breath or unwashed nethers."

"Do you have all those things?"

For some reason this question threw Daria out of her well-rehearsed, world-weary persona. She cocked her head and looked at me sideways. Maybe there was something to me.

"In my office," she said at last.

"Wow. That's really amazing. I guess businesses send you free samples hoping for a favorable review."

"I have enough condoms in my, excuse the expression, drawers to keep the red-light district of Paris going for a week."

I like plain-looking women. What they lack in movie-star headshot style, they make up for in intensity. I think maybe my posture and tone imparted these predilections to the young, pseudo-jaded editor.

"Excuse me, ladies and gentlemen," a voice over the loud speakers said. "My name is Trina MacDonald—"

Before she could continue, the audience broke out into loud applause and cheers. A few people rose to their feet; Mona did.

This was a mild shock to me. Here I had never even heard the name Trina MacDonald and my wife of twenty-two years stood to applaud her. I wondered, if I were to receive an award for assembler language programming, would she get up out of her chair, slap her hands together, and call out for everyone to hear.

"Thank you, thank you," Trina MacDonald's amplified voice boomed. "Please sit down. This is too much, really. *Diablerie* is just another periodical aimed at the heart of America."

There was some polite laughter and the people who had risen returned to their seats.

"Tonight is not about fund-raising or rabble-rousing or vying for power in the White House. You, every one of you here tonight, have been invited to celebrate the start of this oh-so-important publication . . ."

She said more but the renewed applause drowned out the words.

After the ovation subsided, she spent the requisite time thanking the people without whom this undertaking would have, could have, never gotten off the ground. When their names were called out, those people stood to be adored by the crowd. Mona was singled out. So was Daria.

This social business taken care of, Trina, a fiftyish and in-shape woman clad in a form-fitting, green sequined gown, got serious.

"*Diablerie* is a really good time. Our stories are about the world today, about how to get ahead and stay there without going mad. It also covers some of the stories about people who were given up for lost but who made it back by resuscitating themselves when the monitor had gone flatline. One of those women is Barbara Knowland. She was lost in the sex-crazed, drug-filled nightmare that has destroyed so many misguided, self-medicating Americans.

She was accused of murder and nearly convicted when a series of lucky events kept her from a long life in prison. But it was this terrible possibility that woke Barbara up. She decided to get straight and write about that life, to use her experiences to deliver her from depravity. I can only hope *Diablerie* will be able to do the same thing for its readers.

"Ladies and gentlemen, Barbara Knowland."

Trina held out a hand and a woman rose from a table up front. It was a short woman in a blue dress. Star.

The peacock shawl fluttering behind her, Star ascended the stairs to the podium. She and Trina kissed and then the publisher left the stage like an aging movie star who had just passed her mantle into younger, abler hands.

Star was carrying a folded square of paper that she placed on the podium. Then she went about moving the microphone down so that it would accommodate her shorter stature. She unfolded the paper, looked at it, looked up, squinting at the spotlight, and then down at the audience.

She took in a quick breath, as if she was about to speak, but no words immediately followed.

"My name is Barbara," she said at last, "but for more than twenty years I was known as Star. One dictionary I looked up that word in said, I quote, 'a pinpoint of bright light in the darkness.'" She looked around. The audience was completely silent. "That was me. I lived on communes with virgins and murderers. I sold sex in the cities for men I called my boyfriends. I carried drug-filled condoms in my stomach across fifteen borders, and I was tethered by a chain to the back of a truck while Leon Cargill raped, murdered, and dismembered men, women, and children right there next to me."

24

She stopped for a moment then. Maybe others thought that she was experiencing pain from those appalling memories, but I didn't think so. I had met the real Barbara, Star. The woman who chided me for forgetting some long-ago tryst was not going to show real weakness. You could see that in her small, bicolored eyes.

"And then just when I thought the nightmare was over, the police charged me for the crimes. For a while there, when they thought Leon was too crazy to stand trial, they wanted to make me the mastermind. They speculated about my death sentence in the daily papers in Memphis. They found blood on my clothes and in my shoes. They said all kinds of terrible things about me. That's when I turned to Buddhism, when I started meditating."

Barbara/Star reached under the wood podium and came out with a small bottle of water. She guzzled from this. No sipping or tasting for her—no, she turned the bottle upside down with her lips wrapped around the mouth and emptied three quarters of the contents.

"And do you know what Buddha told me through his teachings? That I had created my own hell. I was selling my body and turning a deaf ear to criminal activities. I *was* guilty. Me. I hadn't done what they said. But karma does not distinguish like a court of law. I deserved what I got. Maybe I deserved worse. That's why I've written this book . . ."

"What's wrong, Benny?" Mona asked me on our walk back home.

I was guilty. The words echoed in my mind like the lyrics to a song that you halfway remember for the first time in many years.

"Nothing, Moan."

"That's not my name."

"*Benny*'s not my name. At least I don't introduce you to people as 'Moan Valeria.' "

"Is that what's wrong with you?"

"Have you fucked Harvard Yard yet?" I asked her.

"What?" She was laughing.

She stopped but I kept moving, so she grabbed my sleeve to make me pause.

"What?" she asked again. "Am I hearing right? Ben Arna Dibbuk is jealous?"

"What of it? You drag me out there and make me sit through all that egotistical nonsense while every chance you get you're putting your hands on him, looking at him, fawning over him with all those questions about when he was a cop, when he got shot . . ."

I could see in Mona's eyes a tinge of fear. This was odd because the laughter was there too.

I realized that I must have been getting loud or intense or something.

"I'm sorry, honey," she said softly, attempting to placate me.

I wanted to say more but my breath was confused. I couldn't inhale deeply or exhale enough. It's like the air was stuck in there and I didn't know how to move it around.

My breathing was proof of the rage she feared. Maybe I was angry, but I didn't know why. I hadn't thought about Mona flirting with Harvard Rollins. I just said that because I was tired of her calling me Benny. I certainly hadn't felt jealous. *I was guilty* kept reverberating in my mind.

"Are you okay, Ben?"

"We're gonna do it tonight," I said with absolute certainty.

"Do what?" she asked, but she knew exactly what I meant.

"Fuck you in your ass."

★ ★ ★

The shadow contained a mountain, that much I was sure of. But knowledge without visual corroboration is like a star on a cloudy night: You know it's there but you don't know where—not exactly. In the dream the deep shade was a flat plane against my senses. I would take a tentative step forward and then stop, afraid of falling over some precipice (hadn't I used that word the day before?).

Echoes came to me in staccato, irregular intervals. Sharp rocky crags cut my face and arms, thighs and buttocks (I was naked). The fear of falling made me anticipate the crunching of my skull bones on some rocky floor.

But still I pushed along, listening to the garbled, disjointed echoes for some guidance.

"Ben," she said from behind the flat plane of darkness.

"Star?"

"Do you remember that pipe? The mud on your chest? Do you see me?"

And then I was at my desk at work. I took a deep breath. I must have sighed in my sleep. Work again. My tiny office stacked high with oversize computer printouts in red plastic folders with the program names written on the sides of the reams the way I used to write my name at Louis Pasteur Junior High School in L.A. in the early seventies. *HISTORY, GEOGRAPHY, ALGEBRA,* I wrote on the neatly bound and cut pages of my textbooks. Sometimes I never opened those books, but I labeled them, I knew what they were.

It was then that I noticed the tiny ant wandering purposefully over the coffee-stained printout of DB101SUBROUMSTR, the main program for Our Bank's nightly check-balancing routine.

27

The ant inspected the coffee stain, sprawled like a series of veins across the printed page, but it moved on to a crumb of Starbucks coffee cake. The crumb was much larger than the ant but still the ant lifted it and staggered away toward the edge of the desk.

I was amazed at the ant's might and purpose and relieved that I was no longer under the shadow of that beckoning, unseen mountain. So I watched the tiny creature instead of finding the bug in 101 . . . MSTR.

As the ant went over the edge, I noticed that there were lines of the small creatures moving all over my office, thousands upon thousands of them. They roved the printouts and metal filing cabinets. They were on the window swarming over a slice of Mona's birthday cake that I had put there and forgotten to eat.

Mona cried out then as she did before, when I penetrated her rectum.

"What's my name?" I whispered into her ear.

"Benny," she cried. "BennyBennyBennyBenny . . ."

The rage between us was sex right then. The birthdays forgotten again. The party and Harvard Yard and Star . . . Star.

Ants covered the whole floor when I looked back. My vision became clearer the longer I watched. After a while it was as if I was watching them under a magnifying glass. Their faces were quite human and every one of them wore a top hat cut at a rakish tilt. They each had a piece of birthday cake in their mouth and were moving in communal rhythm as if they were singing. I concentrated on trying to hear them. Then suddenly one of the little revelers burst into flame.

I looked around the office from one ant to another and every insect I gazed upon caught fire and danced a wild ballet of pain.

"Stop! Stop!" a minuscule voice shouted.

I noted then a small ant (the one I first saw on my desk, I was sure) had climbed up onto the magnifying glass that I now realized I was holding. Somehow the lens also amplified its petite voice.

"Your eyes!" the ant shouted. "They're burning my friends. Stop looking at them."

I wanted to do what the ant told me; I intended to stop, but a fascination with fire kept me looking from one ant to another, killing them with my eyes. Then I noticed that the program printouts and their red plastic files had begun to burn. I ran from my office, but it was too late. Fire was everywhere.

"There's no escape," the First Ant said. "You can run and burn or cook where you stand. All those years working and gathering gone up in flames, gone up in flames."

I awoke with a start. Mona was rolled up into a ball as far on her side of the bed as she could manage. The open bottle of Vaseline sat on her night table—mute witness to our grinding carnal abandon.

I took a shower and then went to the kitchen. It was 3:27 when I got there. I wasn't tired, and even if I had been, I doubt that I would have gone back into the inferno of my dreams.

"What do you think it means?" Dr. Shriver might have asked in our weekly session.

I would have made up something and he'd shake his head ever so slightly. And then it would be over: the dream, its possible meanings, our session, another day—a tidy little system of lies like a cheap dime novel from the old days.

I read a lot when I was a teenager. My mother is a reader. My father, before he died, prided himself on reading a book every week. But I had given up that habit somewhere along the way; I lost interest in the narrative line. Everything in a novel leads somewhere. There's a plot and a story and characters that make discoveries. None of that is pleasing to me. That's not the way life works. Life, I thought then, was infinitely tedious or depraved. I wrote down hexadecimal computer code, day in and day out. Mona flitted from one silly magazine to another. There was no plot, no resolution, revelation, character development—or even any change other than the fact that we got older.

I think my parents might have been upset that I no longer read, but I hadn't seen either one of them for many years, even before my father passed on. I would have gone to his funeral but the old banking system, the one I maintained, crashed two nights before the funeral and I had to work seventy-two hours straight in order to set it right.

At least he had come east to see Seela. At least that.

I often thought that I should go out west again but I got tired even thinking about it. My mother's house is too small to stay in; I could have stayed in a hotel, but the traffic in L.A. is awful and room rates are way too high.

Anyway, my mom would be appalled at me not reading.

It didn't seem as if I was missing anything by giving up books, except at times like that morning, when turning on the TV would have awakened Mona. I could have read in the late night hours after nightmares and before the dawn, but I was out of practice.

"Ben?"

It was a little after five. The sun was a glowing promise out beyond Long Island somewhere.

"Yeah, babe."

Mona was wearing only her panties but she held her hands in front of her breasts when she stood before my east-facing throne. I

30

had made her shy with my aggressive sexual appetite. I had made her hurt and bleed but she had also had powerful orgasms and put deep scratches into my left forearm.

I reached for her. It was a quick motion, and before she could move away, I pulled her down into my lap. She fell against me as if she had no bones at all and cried for a very long time—forlorn bleating like a nocturnal beast that had lost its mother to the night.

I don't think that we had ever been closer, that there was ever so much love between us. We hadn't spoken hardly at all since coming back from the party. I came at her and she froze, wanting me and not wanting me.

"Are you okay?" I asked when the sun had become a red ball on the horizon.

"I was afraid of you," she replied. "I wanted to say no but I was afraid of what you might do."

"Have I ever raised my hand to you or Seela?"

"You didn't see that look in your eye. It was like you, like you hated me."

"I don't hate anybody," I said, thinking, *nor do I love or fear or worry about anyone.*

"You hated me last night. You pulled my hair and hurt me."

"I thought you always said you wanted me to be like that, to take you like that."

"I know I said it," she said, "but I didn't really mean it . . . at least not like that. I wanted you to love me, not come at me making those sounds and, and hurting me."

"I'm sorry," I said, now stroking her hair. "I guess I got carried away. Here, let me put you back in the bed."

I stood up holding her in my arms and carried her into the bedroom. While putting her down, I got the intense desire to

31

ravage her again. The passion invaded my breathing so I turned away quickly.

"Aren't you going to join me, Ben?"

"No. I have to go to the bathroom," I said, the werewolf turning away from his lover as the full moon begins to rise.

I locked the door to the bathroom and sat there trying to calm down.

Mona was right. I should have gone back to Dr. Shriver but I was worried what we might find. Maybe I had some chemical imbalance that got worse with age. Maybe the next time I'd lose control.

That made me laugh, and laughing was good. The idea of me, Ben Dibbuk, losing control, for even a moment, was ridiculous. I quit smoking on the first try. I stopped drinking and never even missed it.

There was no unrestrained side to me. It was just sex. Good sex. Nasty, low-down, hard-fucking sex. That's not losing control. It's just human.

Mona was deep asleep by the time I was ready to go to work. I came in to kiss her good-bye but her face was buried away in the blankets.

I didn't know it at the time but that was to be my last normal day of work.

I used my electronic key card at the turnstile-type entrance to Our Bank. Then I came to the bank of elevators, where Molly Ammons greeted me.

"Good morning, Mr. Dibbuk," the chubby white woman said. "Smile."

She pressed a red button on the little stand in front of her and the camera eye above her head snapped a photo of me.

I took the express car to the forty-seventh floor, where I used my key card again to open the glass doors that led to my section. My office was just down the hall to the right, but first I had to sign in at the desk there, where Tina Logan sat every morning brushing her hair or chattering on her cell phone. She never said good morning or anything else to me.

~

One morning a few years ago, I walked in while Tina was leaning over with her head on the desk whispering into her cell phone— sharing secrets with her best girlfriend or some new lover. I was having a problem that day. One of the quarterly runs was putting out a totals sheet that didn't balance with the ATM system. I knew that I was supposed to sign in but I didn't. After all, what difference did it make? They already had my key-card code and picture.

So I went to my office and pulled down the red file for the quarterly master and started reading through the code.

Two hours later there came a knock on my doorless door frame.

"Ben?"

It was Cassius Copeland, maybe the only man in America who had been born after Cassius Clay's first stunning victory over Sonny Liston and named for that champion before he changed his name to Muhammad and then KO'd Liston a second time with the famed "phantom punch."

"Hey, Cass," I said. "What's happening?"

"You, my brother," the dark-skinned security expert intoned.

Cassius's uniform was black trousers and a tight-fitting black turtleneck sweater-shirt that showed off his well-developed physique. He took a stack of red folders off my visitor's chair, threw them into a corner, and sat down.

There was no disrespect in these actions. Cass knew that I had a finely honed sense of my messy office, that I would be able to find any program folder whenever I needed to.

"Me?"

"Uh-huh." He held up a blue slip of paper.

"For me?" I asked, really surprised.

"Tina Logan says that you refused to sign in. She says she asked you but you just shined her on and walked by."

"She had her head on the desk," I said. "And she was talking to her girlfriend or somebody on the phone."

"You want me to write up a slip on her?" Cass offered.

"I don't know why she even works here," I said. "Why do we need a key card, a camera photo every day, and a sign-in sheet? You told me yourself that none of it makes any difference if somebody really wants to mount an attack."

Cassius Copeland smiled enigmatically. His dark features were more compelling than handsome. His eyes seemed like they held a trove of forbidden knowledge.

"Security," he said. "They asked me to set up a security system and that's just what I've done."

"But we're not any safer now than we were before nine-eleven and all these procedures."

"Not safer," Cass said, holding up a powerful, instructive finger, "but more secure."

"What's that supposed to mean?"

"Security, Ben, is a feeling. You got your security blanket, your good-luck charm, your friend on the phone saying you're all right when everything around you is goin' to hell. That's what they hired me for."

"They hired you so that no mad bomber comes in here and blows them all to hell."

"And I promise you, Ben, nobody is gonna blow up the main offices of Our Bank." Cass smiled and I laughed with him.

He tore up the blue slip and dropped it on my overflowing trash can.

From that day on, I signed in every morning at Tina's desk and never felt the slightest bit put out by the absurd security precautions implemented by Cassius Copeland for Our Bank.

~

That morning I was a little sluggish, but coming to work soothed my inflamed emotions from the night and day before. Seela would move into her roach-ridden apartment, Mona would heal from the sex she always asked for but never wanted, Barbara Knowland would move on to another banquet, shocking people with her tales of atrocity and recognizing people from her promiscuous past; people who didn't remember her. And I would sit in that tiny, doorless office copying numbers and making notes that were too boring for anyone else to consider.

When I first came to work at Our Bank, then named New Yorker Savings and Trust, there were sixteen people in my department. I was a lowly entry-level programmer working in COBOL and learning assembly language from an old Irish duffer named Junior. That was way back before PCs and the Internet. We still used information punched into cards and monitors that only had one color—green.

The systems I maintained were developed in the early sixties. There were hundreds of poorly thought-out, poorly executed, almost completely untested programs that broke down every other week. I learned from fixing logic flaws, bugs, in those programs. I wrote obscure subroutines to make up for the faulty logic rife throughout the data processing systems.

The work I did was cutting edge back then, twenty-three years ago, but today all my knowledge is archaic, troglodytic. Nowadays people have laptop computers and swap mountains of information across the fiber-optic Internet highway faster than anyone can monitor.

Over the years, my coworkers died, retired, moved on to different jobs, transferred and learned new systems that came into vogue and then faded away like rap stars and reality-TV celebrities. My department winnowed down and down until only I was left.

Every year a new systems manager comes in and tells me that he, or she, wants to "migrate the system" to a newer database that will allow more-modern computers and computer systems to take over. But banks are conservative places in spite of their new friendly names. My systems mull over hundreds of millions of dollars every night. My salary is in the very low six figures and I'm the only employee. A new computer system would cost millions. And the glitches and bugs in the transition would also be quite pricey. So all I have to do is have a well-documented job sheet so that if I drop dead they can hire an expert just like me (for twice the salary) to keep the old programs running well into the twenty-first century.

I spent the day locating a bug in an old assembler program. It was a branch-and-load-register command that compensated with the wrong command length, found a valid op-code in the data field, and went on its merry way, ignoring all the carefully laid plans of my predecessors.

I fixed the problem and felt fine. It was a good day and I hadn't spoken a word to anyone. Most of the people on my floor didn't know who I was. The only person I answered to, Brad Richards, worked on the sixty-second floor and rarely bothered with me because I did my job, did not complain, and never asked for a raise.

When I got home, there was a note left for me on the butcher-block dining table off the kitchen.

Ben,

My mother called this morning and asked if I could come take care of her. She's got bronchitis and the doctor told her to stay in bed for two days. Call me there after six on my cell.

We should talk when I come home.

Love you,

Mona

I read the note through twice, three times, put it down on the sink, got some ice water from the refrigerator, drank that, and then read the short but pregnant message again.

Why hadn't she called me at work? That was the main question in my mind. She could have asked me what I was going to do for dinner, if I wanted to help her with her mother. And what was this "We should talk"? Was she mad about the night before? She never asked me to stop. I would have backed off if she had only said "no more."

I didn't mind that she wasn't home. I liked being left alone to stare out the window. Many nights Mona went to events with magazine clients. She was often sent out of town to do research or conduct interviews. But there had never been just a note on the table.

I didn't love Mona. But then again, I didn't love anyone: not my parents, who were like strangers after I came to New York; not Seela, though I was very fond of her; not Svetlana. I didn't feel bad about my lack of feeling for Mona because I wasn't secretly giving love somewhere else.

We weren't passionate but at least we were civilized. We took walks together and raised Seela well. We ate a sit-down dinner every night we were both in the house.

And now there was just a note on the dinette table.

It was five to six and so I called her cell phone.

"Hello?" she said in her clipped, I'm-in-a-hurry tone.

"Hey, honey? What's going on?"

"Oh . . . Ben."

"Yeah. How come you didn't call me?"

"Didn't you see my note?"

"You usually call."

"I was in a hurry."

"The phone is faster and better than a note," I said.

"I was upset," she confessed.

"About what?"

"Ben, I have to take care of my mother and I have a new assignment at work. I'm going to be busy all night and for the next few days. So can we put this on hold for a while?"

"Just tell me what's wrong. It's only a few words. A sentence. You're married to a man for over twenty years, have a daughter with him, and you can't spare a few words?"

She sighed as if greatly put upon and then said, "I can't do this. I have to go," and disconnected the call.

I pressed the redial button but the call went directly to her answering service.

You have reached Mona Valeria. I cannot take your call right now. Please leave a number or call back.

It was only after I threw the cordless unit down, shattering it on the kitchen tiles, that I realized how enraged I was. And there was something else: I wanted a drink.

This also was something new. I never wanted a drink. Never in all the years after I went off alcohol. I craved cigarettes aplenty, but it wasn't until after that phone splintered on the floor that I looked around, the way I used to do, for a bottle with a government seal on its neck.

"Hello," she answered sweetly.

"Hi, Lana," I said.

"Ben." In the silence after my name I thought I might have heard a hesitation. But I was so upset that I had no room to contemplate any new suspicions.

I was using Mona's home-office phone.

"I need to come over, baby," I said.

"Sure. Now?"

"If you don't mind."

"It's your house too. You could come here and live with me if you wanted."

The thing about Svetlana was that she was what I called "emotopathic." She could read the feelings rolling off almost anyone and say the things that they needed to hear.

She didn't want me to come live with her. She didn't pretend that there was any more to our relationship than there was. She only knew that she heard loneliness in my tone and so she made up a happy little family for us—her and me together in a tiny studio on the West Side.

★　　★　　★

39

I made it to her place in a little under forty-five minutes. Rush hour traffic meant I had to ride the subway instead of getting a taxi, and the train always takes longer than it should.

I had a key, but I rang from downstairs. She was at her door waiting, looking worried.

"Are you all right?" she asked with that exquisite hint of a Russian accent.

She was wearing the short turquoise dress with the red flecks down the left side. That was my favorite. Her face was made up and I could smell coffee brewing.

Realizing that she had done all that in response to my mournful tone made me a little teary; this in turn disturbed me more—I was losing control and there seemed to be nowhere I could turn.

"Oh, darling," Svetlana said, and she put her arms around my neck, thrusting her small breasts against me.

I stood there, trying to find a way into that embrace, a place that would allow me to yield to an open heart.

"Lana," I said after coffee and sex.

"Yes, my darling."

"What did I say that night?"

She didn't ask me what night. She knew. Our moments together were more predictable than a timetable. There was only one night that stood out.

"I don't remember—not exactly. Why?"

"I don't remember anything," I said, "except that you were asking me something and then I was standing there and you were on the floor."

"I asked you about when you were a child in California."

"And what did I say?"

Svetlana sat up in the bed and hunched over, her large, pointed nipples just touching her slender thighs. As I watched her body, I began to feel nervous, uneasy.

"You said . . . let me see, you said, 'It was all a long time ago and there's nothing anyone can do about it,' and then you threw me."

"I threw you?"

She nodded, the pain of the fall reflected in her face.

"I didn't just stand up and send you sprawling out?" I asked.

"No," she said, shaking her head. "You, how do you say, heav-ed me like a sack of wheat. You went down and came up pushing your arms out."

Svetlana hit me with the palms of her hands, pushing me over on my side in the bed. Then she crawled up on top of me and licked my face like a friendly cat.

"I liked it," she said in a deeper voice. "The next night I masturbated four times thinking about how strong you were."

I was simultaneously aroused and petrified. Svetlana's almost masculine admission, her leaning there on top of me, reminded me of something that, at the same time, I could not remember. It was naked desire with none of the little modesties and lies that I was used to.

"Fuck me, Ben. Do it right now."

In the morning Svetlana was already up and dressed in T-shirt and jeans when I roused sleepily.

"What time is it?" I asked.

"Go back to sleep. It is early."

"No, no. I'll go."

"No," she said. "You don't have to. This is your house. I am your woman. You can stay in my bed. Why not?"

41

"You goin' swimming at the gym?" I asked, just to be saying something, trying to feel like I belonged.

"Yes. Then I go to class. Will you stay again tonight?"

There was something in her voice, or maybe it was in my mind, something that was asking more out of me. The expectation, hers or mine, exhausted me and I fell back into a troubled slumber.

In my dream Barbara "Star" Knowland was standing before a medieval room with a thousand tables. There were acrobats and clowns, jugglers and fire-eaters. One man was selling whole, full-feathered ducks; a dozen of them were hanging by their necks from a bloody cutting board that was somehow attached to the man's chest. He had a crazed look in his eye and an evil curved blade in his left hand.

"That's what you call a dead duck, huh, son?" my father joked.

"Dad?"

He was there at the table and so was my mother, Svetlana, Seela, Mona, a man I had never met before, and Cassius Copeland. The strange man, a white guy wearing a cowboy hat, was looking off toward the back of the room, which was very far away.

My parents were sitting side by side, deep satisfaction radiating from them. They loved each other. They loved me—they said. I sat there watching them and feeling that I was somehow in that faraway distance that the stranger at our table was looking into.

The man I didn't know turned to me and asked, "Are you interested in real estate, Ben Dibbuk?"

"What kind of real estate?" I asked, wondering why he used my full name. Why not say "Ben" or "Mr. Dibbuk"? I was stuck thinking about his use of my name when Barbara Knowland began speaking.

"I've seen thousands of people die," she announced. "I've seen them shot and hacked, knifed and blown up, poisoned and beaten to death with steel batons. I've seen whole towns annihilated, countries decimated by famine. I've walked through infirmary halls with the smell of death so thick that if you cut it with a knife, it would bleed all over you."

Everyone was rapt in her hypnotic hyperbole.

What nonsense! I thought.

But the man I didn't know leaned over and whispered, "Only the innocent can deny sin, my friend." Then he gave me his card. The name was written in runes but the title *Cowboy* was in plain type.

I got to work five minutes early. I was about to use my card on the turnstile when someone called to me.

"Ben."

It was Star, standing near the coffee concession that made its business out of a nook in the east wall of the huge entrance hall.

She was wearing dungarees and a tie-dyed T-shirt of mainly purple and yellow. Her hair was down and she wore no makeup.

For a moment I thought I recognized her from another time, but that flash of insight faded.

I stayed where I was and she approached me.

"Ben."

"What?"

"You're still saying that you don't know me?"

"Lady, I don't have the slightest idea who you are," I said. "I saw you the night before last. I read a review of your book online . . . but I don't know you."

"We spent almost twenty-four hours living on whiskey and sex," she said. Her green eye seemed to shimmer while her brown one receded.

"What can I say? I did that a hundred times when I was drinking and rambling around."

"Why did you come to my talk?" she asked.

"I told you. My wife is working for *Diablerie*."

"I know. I called her office. I asked her why she brought you and she said that you usually didn't come to things like that."

"Did she also tell you that she made me go this time?"

"What are you up to, Ben?" Star asked. "Are you trying to hurt me? Do you want something?"

"No. No. I don't even know you."

Once again the suspicion shone in her face. She backed away a few steps and then turned. She walked a few steps more and turned again.

It all seemed very dramatic, histrionic.

She left and I went up to work.

There were a few lines of code in a tax percentage program that I had to modify almost every year because of ever-changing tax laws. I wanted to work on the subroutine but there was too much on my mind: Mona's abandonment, Lana's openness, and now Star's paranoia. Maybe I should have asked her what happened all those years ago. Maybe I should have pretended that I remembered her, that I missed her.

But why bother? What could she do to me?

I couldn't imagine any danger she might present but still I was uneasy, panicky even. I tried to concentrate on the printouts but for once they gave me no solace. I couldn't hide behind the jury-rigged logics, the objective commands that were perfectly precise but often wrong.

I was lost that day, but I told myself this feeling would pass. Over time Mona would come back home and Star Knowland didn't matter. Whatever she remembered, or thought she remembered, was more than twenty years ago and a thousand miles away.

At noon I gave up trying to work. I called my manager, Brad Richards, got his answering machine, and said, "Hey, Brad. This is Ben Dibbuk. I have some kind of virus or something so I'm going home. I should be better by tomorrow."

I hadn't been free on the street before five on a workday in years. I went out to lunch with Cassius every now and then, but that was always with the idea of coming back to work.

At first I walked toward our apartment because that's what I did every day. But somewhere around Forty-ninth Street I realized that the apartment would be lonely without Mona.

Lonely without Mona. The words swirled in my head, holding other meanings. I never missed Mona. She could go out every night for weeks, and often did, and I never felt lonely. She was once working in San Francisco for three months, getting a new publication off the ground, and we barely called each other once a week.

But now, after less than a day, I was missing her.

I headed south. I had a destination, but not consciously. It wasn't until I got to Thirty-sixth Street that I realized I had been headed for Maria Valeria's apartment building.

Maria's husband, Isaac, had died when Mona was only eight. He and Maria had come from Jamaica in order to make a new life. They loved their daughter and even now Maria stayed in New York to be near Mona.

45

I rang the bell downstairs even though I knew Mona would be angry at my just showing up. But I missed her; I wanted to see her.

No one answered and I thought that I should leave and call her on her cell phone. But I had the keys to Maria's apartment in my pocket. Mona made me carry them in case she was out of town and there was an emergency.

I opened the downstairs door thinking that I'd knock, in case the bell was broken.

No one answered. I stood there a moment, knocked again, looked at my watch—it was 1:21 and I had nowhere to go.

I opened the door telling myself that Mrs. Valeria was sick with bronchitis, maybe she'd fallen or had some kind of asthma attack.

But the apartment was empty. The kitchen was clean. Maria's bed was made and neat. There were no medicine bottles on the night table or extra blankets at the foot of the bed, no humidifier or oxygen tent, no evidence of respiratory illness at all.

The guest bedroom also doubled as Maria's office. It was where she knitted and wrote letters on a wobbly cherry table/desk that I had made when I was studying woodworking at the Y.

Mona's little satchel was at the foot of the bed. It was obvious that she just wanted to get away from me for a while. Maria wasn't sick.

I knew that I should leave, but Mona's desertion of our home, her lie about her mother's illness, made me suspicious. That's why I emptied her satchel out on the bed.

A toothbrush, her favorite yellow towel, cartridges for the Mont Blanc Mozart fountain pen, aspirin, Ambien, and a package of six ribbed condoms were arrayed on her neat blankets.

It was not possible for me to explain away those condoms. We hadn't used them for years. Her tubes were tied after Seela. The pregnancy was so hard on her that we both decided to be happy with one child.

Mona had a lover somewhere. For how long? Had it started with that trip to San Francisco? Was it only one, or was it many lovers?

Little hints came back to me as I knelt there next to the bed so as not to muss her tightly tucked covers. For a while she had talked during our nightly dinners about a man named Tom Inch. He was a journalist, and she let it slip one day that they had gone to see a film while in Las Vegas at a convention.

I was a little bothered by this and said so.

"It was nothing," she told me. "We were doing a profile on that young actress Jessa Sterling. She had a small role in the film. It was just business."

I forgot about it before dessert.

Then there was another guy, I had forgotten his name. He was an artist, I remembered, and used to call the house. They had long talks on her office phone. She laughed loud and hard while talking to him. Once, after a brief talk with the artist, she told me that she was going to her mother's for the evening. I didn't think about it at the time. It seemed . . . ordinary. And I didn't ask a lot of questions.

∼

The image of my father, a giant, came into my mind. Tall and dark-skinned like me, he went up and down the lane beside our house watering the rosebushes—the huge multicolored orange and yellow and red flowers releasing their heavy, sweet scent all around us.

"What if the sun came down on that mountain, Daddy?" I asked.

"It wouldn't do that," he said, watching the stream from the green hose, making sure that he didn't wash the soil away from the roots.

"But what if it did?"

"Probably be a forest fire up there, I guess."

"And what if it was a fire, Daddy?"

"It would burn the trees and the flowers, if there are any flowers up there."

"And if it was flowers, they would burn?"

"I guess."

"What if all the flowers burnded up, Daddy?"

"The bees would have trouble makin' honey, honey."

I giggled and asked, "And what if the bees couldn't make their honey?"

The whole afternoon was spent asking one question after another. Remembering that I knew there was a time when I questioned everything.

~

There came a sound: the front door of the apartment opening. I scooped Mona's things into her bag, put it where I found it, and tiptoed into the closet, closing the louvered door behind me.

I was sure that it was Mrs. Valeria coming home from the market. She would putter around for a while and then go out again. That's how Maria spent her days—in and out of the house, going on made-up errands. All I had to do was wait until the front door opened and closed again; it wouldn't be more than an hour—probably less.

They came through the bedroom door kissing. Their heads locked together as they twisted into the room. His erection was out and in her hand. His hand was under her skirt, the forearm jerking upward and turning again and again.

"Oh, yeah," Mona said, the orgasm teasing behind her panting breaths. "Right up in there. Deeper. Oh. Hold it right there. Don't move. Don't move."

She was on her toes, biting her lower lip, her eyes closed. A high-toned squeal escaped her throat.

"Kiss that cock," Harvard Rollins said.

She looked at him then. I knew what she'd say. Mona hated it when men talked like that. "Gutter mouth," she called it.

"You want me to take that big dick down my throat?" she asked him.

He took her by the shoulders and threw her to the floor. She fell like a rag doll, her dress dropping away from her shoulders. She came right up on her knees and went at his long, slender erection hungrily. Her face was hidden from me but I could tell that she was looking up at him. He stared down at her lovingly. Every now and then he'd make a hissing sound, letting us both know how wonderful she made him feel.

She held his manhood away from her lips and said, "I can taste your come. Hold it back."

As Mona stood up, her striped dress fell away from her slender hips. She wore no underwear. Then she turned her back to him and leaned over to reach into her little leather bag.

I froze, worried that she might see the jumble of her things and realize I had gone through it. But she didn't.

"I have a condom in—" she began to say, but Harvard moved quickly, sinking the entire length of his stiff erection inside her.

"Oh my God," she cried. "Oh my God."

49

Harvard was fucking her hard while holding on to one of her wrists. Every time he slammed into her, she almost lost her balance, almost came, while he somehow kept her from falling, kept her panting.

"I'm coming!" he shouted.

Mona turned around quickly and got back on her knees. She grabbed his thing and stroked it and he began to ejaculate. As the long streams leaped from the snakelike head of his pink erection, Mona laughed and urged him on. Even after it was over, she kept pulling on it.

"Come again," she begged. "Come for me. Show me you love me. Do it again."

For a moment I was sure that he was going to push her away, but then he bent over, lifted her by her waist, and put her on the table I had made. He entered her again and repeated his exuberant pounding. The slapping of flesh was like one man's hearty applause in a room full of doubters.

The poorly made table rocked and squealed along with Mona. She was cheering, shouting, screaming, "Fuck me goddammit! Fuck me!"

I wondered many things in my dark closet. The only light brought images of my beautiful middle-aged wife, wanton with passion for a man I hardly knew.

I wondered why I wasn't aroused by the sexuality and why I wasn't angry at either of them. I hypothesized on whether or not Mona had used that kind of language with all men but me. And I thought about Harvard Rollins; had he been her lover long?

"Oh yeah," Harvard said; it was almost a whisper. "Oh God, yeah. Here it comes." He doubled, then tripled, his already frenzied beat. Mona was singing a wordless song of praise. She got louder and louder while Harvard just kept hammering away. When he finally came, he emitted three hard grunts. Mona sat up, using her well-defined abs, and stared longingly into his eyes.

They stayed in that position for some time, gazing at each other, tremors going through their bodies at odd moments.

After maybe two more minutes he lifted her again and carried her to the bed.

They lay side by side and she kissed him carelessly, something she had never done with me. With me her kisses were always short and accurate. With Harvard you had the feeling that she wanted to lick his face.

I thought about Lana then, her licking me.

"What are we going to do about Ben?" she asked Harvard.

"I don't know yet," he replied in a matter-of-fact tone. "Tell ya the truth, I find it hard to believe."

"But maybe he did. Maybe we never knew each other."

A laugh deep inside me strained to get out. The idea that I was in their conversation and in the closet at the same time seemed too bizarre. I wanted to walk out casually as my wife held Harvard's now flaccid penis, to sit on the bed and make some wisecrack.

"Do you think he has a lover?" Harvard asked.

"He's not interested in sex," she said dismissively. "Never was, really. He never let go, not even in the beginning. You know how it is. Some men think because they can get it up that women love it."

"But you said that you might not really know him."

"Yeah," she said. She sat up and leaned over to kiss the head of his cock. "It's so beautiful."

"Are you sure you want me to do this?"

"Fuck me?"

"Look into Ben's past."

"Fuck me first," she said.

I didn't watch the next two bouts of lovemaking. I sat back in the closet while Mona moaned and Harvard grunted, wondering why my wife would want to investigate me. She'd said that she didn't think I had lovers. She was wrong about that, but if that wasn't her worry, what was?

I was beginning to feel fear in that closet. What was happening to me? Why was my past, a past that held nothing but a few drunken benders, coming back?

There was nothing to worry about. I hadn't done anything but have an affair with a young Russian student.

Still the threat of Harvard Rollins looking into my past made me wish I had a weapon. I thought about holding a pistol in my hand. This thought was so alien and yet so natural that I began to fear my own response. What was wrong with me?

When the door to the bedroom closed, I realized that I had stopped paying attention to the lovers. A moment later the front door to the apartment opened and closed. I could have left then. I should have left before Mrs. Valeria returned, but I stayed in the dark wondering why my innocuous past had become so important.

I felt safe in the darkness. From there I could watch and still remain hidden. Maria could have come home and never once looked behind that door. In the night, while she slept, I could sneak out and get water and food. I wondered semi-seriously how I could make a life like that—hidden.

On the train ride up to Lana's place I was going over the past few days with Mona. She had been talking about divorce, had been thinking about the settlement. She believed I didn't have a lover and so she needed Harvard Rollins to help her prove her case against me. Of course that was it. It wasn't my past but her need to somehow incriminate me that made Mona turn to Rollins.

Maybe when she had talked to Barbara Knowland, she came up with the idea to find out about my wild drunken days in Colorado. Now it was making sense. She wanted to make sure she could prove that I was the bad guy before suing for divorce. Of course.

"Ben, Ben, Ben, Ben," Lana cried over and over as we made love for the third or fourth time that night. While we fucked on the floor next to her bed, I was thinking, couldn't stop thinking about Mona and Harvard Rollins. There was no jealousy to it. I was excited about how she kissed him and how she didn't even complain when he wouldn't wait for her to bring out the condoms. I could see in her face how excited she was that he would not be limited by her.

I was grinding away at Lana even though I knew that I'd had my last orgasm of the night an hour before. But when I thought of the grunting pleasure Mona exhibited while watching Rollins ejaculate, as I watched secretly over her shoulder, I came again—painfully hard. In the middle of that passionate surprise the muscles of my left buttock went into a spasm and I tumbled off Lana and cried out in pain.

"What's wrong, Ben?"

"I got a charley horse in my butt," I said, laughing and groaning at the same time.

Lana rolled me over and began massaging the taut cheek with her elbow. After a minute the pain subsided. As soon as it did, I began feeling excited about her massage.

53

"You have never made love to me like this," Svetlana said as she kneaded my quivering backside.

"I don't know what it is," I said. "Mona stayed away from home and I made a beeline straight to you."

Lana turned me over and looked into my eyes.

"Are you falling in love with me?" she asked.

"I don't know what's happening, baby," I said. "There's something, something wrong. But I don't know what it is. If you had asked me a week ago what I'd be doing with my life in twenty years, I would have told you that Mona and I would be in the same apartment and I'd be at the same job. But now I don't know where I'll be tomorrow."

"Is it because I called you that night?"

"No. I don't know what it is."

"You never make love to me like this," she said again.

"Like what?"

"Like you are hungry for me, like animal. I get afraid a little and I like this and I'm scared too. Maybe when you were biting me, I was feeling a little like I was falling in love."

My heart was pounding but not with the feeling of sex. I was afraid. I closed my eyes, and even though Lana kept talking, I stopped listening. I tried to figure out what had happened, what had scared me so.

It was hard to concentrate. My well-ordered little life had come apart like a flower that drops all its petals after having finished its work. I felt desperate, when only days before life had been parsed out like plain white bread, one slice after the other all exactly the same.

"Maybe we should take a vacation," I said, interrupting whatever it was Lana was saying.

"Where would we go?"

"Maui? Hawaii."

Lana kissed me and then stood up, pulling me toward the bed. When we were under the covers, she sat up on my chest and cupped her hands around my face.

"You mean this?" she asked.

"Yes."

"What will you tell your wife?"

"Nothing. It's none of her business."

Svetlana took a deep breath through her nose and then moved up so that she was straddling my face. My lips and nose were right there next to her sex. I could smell our lovemaking there.

"Make me come again," she said.

The next morning found me walking down through Central Park a little before seven. Every time I stepped forward with my left leg, that testicle hurt with a deep aching that I hadn't experienced in years.

It was early July and hot every day except that morning, which was cool, even a little brisk. Every sound and color was clear and crisp to me; my fingertips were alive at the touch of stone or bark or the thread-textured cloth of my jacket.

I kept slapping my hands together and then rubbing my fingertips. I was muttering to myself about sex and Hawaii, my wife and the sudden and unexpected crash and burn of our marriage.

Seela was old enough to weather the breakup. She had her roaches and her roommate.

Harvard Rollins wouldn't stay with Mona very long but she'd find some minor celebrity to share her bed and accompany her to those interminable magazine parties.

I wanted a drink more than I ever had before in my life. But drinking would kill me, I knew that for sure. I had almost died twice in Colorado before I came out to New York. I'd put my fist through a plate glass shower door, ripping my forearm wide open and bleeding out at least two pints of blood. My neighbor, Charles Dagger, had saved me that time. Then, two months later, I drove my Dodge station wagon off the side of an embankment, totaled the car, and nearly fell down an eighty-foot drop. That's when I decided to leave Colorado.

Drinking brought me to death's door twice; the third time, I was sure, would be my end.

But I still wanted a drink. The mildly citrusy tang of tequila was on my mind. Tequila or cognac, either fruity liquor would do just fine.

I started skipping at every fourth and then fifth step. I wasn't aware of it at first but then I saw people shying away from me. I guess I looked kind of loony. I was a little nuts. But why shouldn't I have been? My life was spiraling from its orbit for no good reason.

Abruptly I stopped to sit on a park bench. I jumped to the seat rather forcefully and the couple sitting there got up and left.

"You don't have to leave," I said after them, but they didn't seem to hear.

What was wrong? How had I gotten to that place with no warning, no diagnosis? I was tapping my left foot and clapping my hands three-quarters off beat. It was a rhythm I had thought up years before, even before I left Los Angeles, but I had never been able to do it. It was a musical exercise and I was in no way musical. But on that bench I could keep up the tempo and even riff off of it, calling out notes again from the offbeat.

I guess I was getting pretty loud when the policeman walked up to me.

"Excuse me, sir," the uniformed and armed cop said. "Is there a problem?"

I lost the cadence and this enraged me. I stood up from the bench, a little too quickly, and said, "No, Officer. What makes you think that?"

"You're creating a disturbance, sir," the officer said, holding his head to the side, searching my eyes for signs of alcohol inebriation or drug use.

"Got a lot on my mind, man. Wife left me yesterday. Twenty-two years and she bolted like a teenage girl."

"Can I see some ID?"

I produced my employment card and the cop studied it.

"You have a license?" he asked.

"Don't drive much. It's in my bureau," I said. "At home."

"Try to keep it down, okay, Mr. Dibbuk? Your behavior is erratic and it's causing some consternation."

It was that last word that made me look closely at the peace officer. A white guy, maybe thirty, maybe not quite; he had light brown eyes and a brutal mouth. I would have bet a hundred thousand dollars that he would have never used the word *consternation*.

"Excuse me, Officer. I'll try to calm down."

The policeman walked away, taking all my nervous energy with him.

When I got home, it was a little after eight fifteen. I wanted to change for work. And even though I was going to be late, I was at peace again. The policeman cured me of my alcohol jones and my worries.

Mona was gone. That part of my life was over. I could accept that. Maybe Svetlana would be a better wife or lover. Maybe I could become a freelance expert in computers and double my salary so that the bite of alimony wouldn't feel so bad.

I walked in and went right to the kitchen. I was looking in the refrigerator for an English muffin when Mona called out, "Ben? Is that you, Ben?"

She came from the bedroom hall wearing the same striped dress that had fallen down around her thighs when she was commenting on the flavor of Harvard Rollins's cock.

I stood there listening to the hard breath blowing through my nostrils. My heart followed with a drumbeat. I imagined the knife on the counter buried in her chest.

All this felt like a second body rising out of the shell that I was: a man who I didn't know, or at least did not remember, rising up to take control.

I held my breath and took a step backward.

"Ben? What's wrong?"

"What are you doing here, Mona?"

"My mother is doing better," she said. "I came home last night."

"Better?"

"Yes. Where were you?"

"I . . . I thought you had left me," I said quite honestly.

"Left you? Just because I went a few blocks away to take care of my mother?"

"You just left a note . . . hung up the phone on me . . ." I wanted to add that she allowed Harvard Rollins to use words that were strictly taboo between us, but I felt that speaking about her infidelity would expose me. I needed to keep my knowledge a secret.

"I was busy," she said. "Is that what you think? That I'd just walk out the door and that would be it?"

"You were talking about divorce the other day at Augie's. You were looking at Harvard Rollins like he was the man of your dreams." Honesty as far as it would go, I decided.

"So where were you?"

"With Cass," I said, realizing that the truth would only take me so far.

"Who's Cass?"

"A guy I work with."

"What were you doing with him?"

"Getting drunk."

"You had a drink? You said that you'd never—"

"So now will you leave me because I had a drink?"

"What's wrong with you, Ben? Why do you keep on saying that I'm leaving you?"

"We got drunk," I said. "I was too wasted even to take a cab, so I stayed at his place."

Mona took a step toward me and I, afraid of the knife on the table and in my mind, took another step back.

"What's wrong, Ben?"

"Why aren't you calling me 'Benny'?"

"You told me that you didn't like it."

"That never stopped you before," I said in the voice of an accusing attorney. "It didn't stop you from introducing me to Harvard as 'Benny.'"

"What's this thing about Harv?" she asked.

"Yeah, that's right, *Harv*," I said. "I'm sure you're on first-name terms with his dick too."

"Don't you use that kind of language with me," she said, suddenly rigid.

"Okay," I said. "Then try this: Fuck you, you cunt."

I walked by her and out the door before anything else could well up out of me. I stormed down the street, walked all the way to work and right past the entrance. I just kept on going toward the west side of town.

I was swinging my arms like some kind of mentally challenged inmate suddenly free on the streets of New York.

That was a Wednesday. Svetlana had classes all day and one at night. She said that she hoped I would be there when she got home. I suppose I could have gone to her house, but I was afraid of my hands and my mind. I was afraid of what I would say or do or allow to be done to me. It was as if I had been possessed by, by . . . Star.

Things began going wrong when I met her. She had claimed that we knew each other, she had called Mona at work—who knows what she had said?

As I came into Times Square I realized that my feet and fingers were numb. This was a familiar feeling but I had forgotten when I had last experienced that sensation.

I stopped at a Starbucks and got a triple espresso. Then I went to a movie starring Bruce Willis. I forget the title—actually I can't even remember the story; there was a lot of screaming and shooting and a few funny moments. I laughed way too loud and the people around me moved away.

Lunch at a French bistro was good. I ordered a glass of red wine but didn't drink it. After I left, I bought a pack of cigarettes. I smoked three of them. I had to have something to see me through that day.

At four o'clock I found myself at Lincoln Center. A guard pointed me to a phone booth at the lower level of the main hall.

I didn't own a cell phone at that time—never thought I needed one. I was rarely anywhere but work or home and I had no close friends. Anyway, cell phone users on the street seemed like idiots to me. Here they had their one chance to be alone and contemplative walking down the street and they'd get on the phone talking to whomever they had just seen or were going to see.

I settled in the phone booth, took a deep breath, and started entering digits. First was the 800 number for my carrier, then the long-distance number I wanted to call. I had to enter my home phone and then a secret PIN before the machine would allow the call to go through.

"Hello," she said in the wary tone that the elderly have whenever they have to deal with the outside world.

"Mom?"

"Ben?" she asked, amazement replacing her caution.

"Yeah, Mom. How are you?"

"Why are you calling me, Ben? Is Mona sick? Is it Seela?"

"I just wanted to say hi, Mom. What's wrong with that?"

"You haven't called here in seven and a half years," she said. I was sure that she could have told me the exact number of days.

"I wanted to talk with you, to ask you some questions."

"You haven't called since before the day I called your house to tell you that your father had died. You never even got on the line. It was Mona that I talked to."

It couldn't have been that long—could it? I remember thinking about calling her on her birthday, more than once.

"You didn't come to the funeral," she said. "You never call, but Mona did last year."

"She did?"

"She said that she was thinking about me. She tried to apologize for you but I told her that I was just happy to have a granddaughter and a daughter-in-law who called now and then."

"I'm sorry, Mom. I wanted to—"

"Your aunt Justine died two years ago," she said.

"I'm sorry to hear—"

". . . so I had to quit my job, because she was my ride to Westwood. I just sit in the house all day now. Your brother's in jail again, but you probably know that. I guess at least you aren't a criminal like Briggs. And I have your father's retirement from the city, and his health insurance. You know I had a knee replacement."

"Are you okay?"

"Not that anyone cares, but I can walk to the Vons on my own. You never even came to your own father's funeral. Briggs at least got a pass from prison . . ."

The void reaching out from my shoulders into my brain carried the taint of a madman in its tendrils. All kinds of obscenities rose up in my throat.

". . . I never thought I'd feel that I regretted my own son's birth but—"

I hung up and walked away from the phone booth. You couldn't blame my mother. She'd only seen me twice in fifteen years and both those times they had come east.

Outside, on Broadway, I lit a Lucky Strike and inhaled deeply, feeling the release of the nicotine. I closed my eyes, let the sun warm my face. There were horns blaring and scuffling feet all around me, voices talking, talking, talking and bird cries. I heard the faraway roar of a jet engine coming in for a landing at La Guardia. A whining siren moved sinuously in my ear, and various slams, rumbles, and hisses arose in my imposed darkness.

I took another hit off the cigarette and the calm went deeper. Nineteen years since I'd had a cigarette. I quit because Mona said that she'd leave me if I continued to smoke around our child.

The killer weed instructed me, composed me. I squatted down on the busy sidewalk, my elbows on my knees and the cigarette between my fingers. I was a solitary scout on a Western plateau, alone and satisfied with life. Far down in the valley, behind my closed eyes, a cloud of dust warned of strangers in my nearly hemispheric domain.

I entered all the codes again. This time another woman answered, "Marston Group."

"Idelle?"

"Yes? Who is this?"

"Ben Dibbuk."

"Oh. Hello, Mr. Dibbuk. How are you?"

"I guess I wouldn't be calling you if I was okay."

"You'd like to make an appointment with Dr. Shriver?"

"Yes, ma'am, I sure would."

"I'll have him call you," she said.

"Thanks," I replied, thinking about inhaling more smoke.

"Jericho Detention Facility," a clipped, efficient male voice declared.

"I need to speak to an inmate," I said. "Briggs Dibbuk."

"Hold on a minute," the voice said.

This friendly turn surprised me. I expected at least a few bureaucratic hurdles at a federal penitentiary.

A few moments later he got back on the line and gave me a number to call.

That number was busy for quite a while. It was a nuisance because I had to enter all those codes to make the San Diego call. Jericho prison was a special detention center for criminals who had turned state's evidence against other, supposedly worse, offenders. It was minimum security and most of that was there to protect the inmates from retaliation by those they had double-crossed.

Briggs had been smuggling heroin from Mexico into Texas. He moved quite a lot of product for highly placed diplomats and military men on both sides of the border. When he got caught, those influential gentlemen allowed my brother to present evidence, that they supplied him with, about lower-level dealers. So Briggs had turned in guilty men with whom he had never worked.

He was happy with his eleven-year sentence.

"Gives me time to reflect," he told me the one time we discussed his situation over the phone. "Maybe I'll get some kinda degree so I won't have to deal drugs no more when I get out."

The phone rang on the fourteenth attempt.

"Jericho eight," a voice answered.

"Briggs Dibbuk," I said.

A space of time elapsed.

"Hello?"

"Hey, Briggs."

"Benny, Ben. Hey, brother. I thought you said that you didn't wanna have anything to do with me."

"I don't. But I need something."

"Why the fuck should I help you when you won't even let me call your house?"

"Because I send you a check for two hundred and fifty dollars every other month," I said. "Because you know you're going to need my help again one day. Because you're my brother and you know why I keep my family away from you."

"Just hurry up, man," he said. "Tell me what you want."

"Do you remember when I left Colorado to come to New York?"

"Yeah."

"Did I call you back then?" I asked, a tremor playing on my diaphragm.

"You mean one'a them midnight rambler calls you was so famous for?"

∾

I hadn't thought about those calls since my drinking days. They were a symptom of the alcohol—the only really hard evidence I had that I was experiencing blackouts.

At first I only phoned my parents in the dead of night from my L.A. apartment and, after that, from Colorado; I would call them, waking them up. I'd blather and cry, curse and condemn them. I could not remember later when they'd tell me about it.

"You call up here usin' all kinds of language," my father would say to me. "Cussin' your mother, tellin' me that I'm the reason you dropped out of college. Sayin' that we hurt you in your mind."

Not long after I moved to Colorado they stopped answering the phone past ten. I think that they must have unplugged it. And so then I began calling my brother. He was just a pot dealer at that time and the police didn't pay much attention to him. He'd call me a few days later and tell me what I'd said. In that way I kept up with myself, my brother being a kind of auxiliary memory device.

~

"Yes," I said. "Did I call you around that time?"

"Uh-huh. You sure did. I remember because it was a collect call. But I didn't think it was one'a your drunk rambles. You sounded stone-cold sober."

"What did I say?"

"You wanted to know how easy was it to get blamed for a crime," Briggs said. He was enjoying the talk now, now that he was in charge.

"What crime?"

"That's what I asked you, but all you would say is, 'Somethin' serious.'"

"What did you tell me?"

"That the best way to catch a man is his fingerprints or an eyewitness."

"What about a witness?" I asked.

"You cussed out some woman, said that she wasn't about to say a thing."

"What woman?" I asked.

"It was a long time ago, bro. I didn't write it down. I figured you stole some shit or somethin' like that. You know you always was small-time. Oh yeah," he said then, "I remember. The woman's name was Star."

The blood felt as if it were congealing in my veins. I slammed my fist down on my knee and ground my teeth until they hurt.

"Are you sure of that?" I asked.

"Oh, yeah. You said, 'that bitch Star,' about a hundred times. I guess that should'a told me it wasn't one'a your rambles. But otherwise you sounded sober as a judge."

I wandered after that for some time. My head ached but the feeling was far-off, inconsequential. Barbara Knowland knew something about me that I myself did not know. I had called my brother and told him that it was a crime. But that was more than twenty years ago. How bad could it have been?

I didn't know.

I thanked God for my Lucky Strikes; without them I might have run out into traffic or down in front of a train.

I woke up with her kissing my ear. She kissed it again and again, cooing softly. I had no idea where I was or whom I was with.

"Ben?"

I turned over to see Svetlana lying next to me.

"Are you better?"

"Better than what?"

"Last night when I came in, you were in the bed crying." She reached out, cupping my jaw with her hand.

"Did I say anything?"

"Not that I could understand. But you were so sad. I held you for a long time."

I sat up, hurting everywhere, it seemed: my face, my chest, my feet from all that walking.

"What time is it?" I asked.

"Ten, a little after."

"Don't you have a class?"

"I did not go," she said. "I was worried about how you felt."

That set off my sobbing again. When I started crying, I

67

remembered the night before; not why, but that I was crying, moaning, sorrowful beyond measure.

Svetlana held me, humming along with the song of lament. Her strong hands were a solace to me but I could not tell her that: I couldn't speak. After what seemed like a long while, she put on her robe and prepared breakfast: cornflakes with skim milk and black coffee.

When I lit a cigarette, she was startled.

"What is this? You are smoking now?" she asked.

"Oh . . . yeah. I need it. I need it bad."

"But you have quit for so long," she said.

"The stuff on my mind is from so long ago that only smoking and drinking can get to it," I said, realizing that there was more truth to those words than I had considered.

"You are drinking too?"

"Not until I'm ready to die," I said.

"Ben," she said, a cry in that deep shadow of my dream. "Ben, why are you so sad?"

"I don't remember."

"What do you mean?"

"My mind," I said. "Something happened a long time ago. Something that I've forgotten. There's a woman who I ran into who knows what that something is. She thinks I remember too. When I told her that I forgot, she got worried."

"Can you ask her what this is?"

"I'm afraid to."

Svetlana's response was a smile, then a toothy grin.

"This is funny to you?" I asked.

"No, darling." It was the first time she had ever called me *darling*. "It is just that you are like a new boyfriend to me. Dark and

68

filled with secrets, smoking at my table and crying in my bed. You are a new man for me, a second secret lover who throws me down on the floor and takes me."

We made love after that. And when we were finished, she kissed me, got dressed, and walked out the door without saying good-bye.

Ten minutes later the phone rang. I answered, certain that she was calling to mend the oversight.

"Yes?" I said into the receiver.

"Who is this?" a man with a heavy Russian accent asked.

"My phone, your name," I said.

The caller hung up. It was no wrong number, surely. The Russian accent meant that it was some friend or acquaintance of Lana's. While I pondered this, the phone rang again.

"Yes?"

"Is Svetlana there?"

"Who's calling?"

"Who are you?"

"My phone. Your name first."

"I am Sergei, Lana's . . . friend."

"I am Ben. I pay for this phone." After these words, I hung up.

There was a cold darkness in me. Not the darkness of race but the moonless night of a hunter looking for warm blood. There was no mistaking the thrumming in my chest. My fingers wanted to close on a throat, any throat.

It wasn't that I felt jealousy. I didn't care if Lana had a "friend." She was young and very pretty. I was getting on toward the later years when the body, mind, and heart start to wind down. I wanted to hurt someone, but not for revenge.

I reached for my Lucky Strikes, but the pack was empty.

★   ★   ★

69

Four blocks away I stopped at a kiosk to buy cigarettes. It was a very small stand that sold chewing gum and newspapers, instant lottery tickets and racing forms. I bought a pack of filterless Camels. Three blocks later I picked up a free copy of the *Village Voice*. I took the paper over into Central Park and sat down at another bench.

It occurred to me that Lana was right. I was a much different man than I had been just a day before. Yesterday I had been all herky-jerky, skipping down the street and lamenting my wife's betrayal. Today I had woken up devastated, blubbering like a child, but now I was as calm as a contract killer on the old TV show *Kojak*, waiting for his next job.

I smoked three cigarettes, found what I was looking for in the performances section of the paper, and watched a big blustering pigeon try time after time to mount shy and reluctant hens.

I wandered around for a long time, finally making it home at a little after three. I was planning to pack a bag and go to a hotel. There was a small place on Thirty-sixth Street, the Reynard, that rented rooms by the week. It wasn't far from Mrs. Valeria's apartment but she'd never know I was there.

I wanted to get in and out quickly but Mona was there sitting on the sofa that faced my river-watching chair. She was wearing a white skirt and a black T-shirt. Her white hair and copper skin made her seem somehow transcendent.

∾

"My ancestors were the Indians who lived in the Caribbean before the Europeans came," she once told me. "They had red skin and straight hair. Not like the slaves."

"But your skin has a lotta brown in there," I said. "And you straighten your hair."

There I was, saying everything she didn't want to hear. No wonder she took lovers.

~

"Hello, Ben."

Without speaking I went into the bedroom, took out my small traveling suitcase, and gathered together my socks and underwear, jeans and shirts.

"Ben." She was standing behind me now, blocking the exit from our small sleeping room.

I snapped the latch on the bag and turned toward her, waiting patiently for her to move aside.

"You can't just walk out like this," she said.

There were rebuttals in my head but my mouth refused to utter them. I looked at her feathery white tresses and soulful deep eyes. She was as much a stranger to me as I was fast becoming stranger to myself. Our actions and words seemed to come from other players, understudies who had completely different takes on the roles of our lives.

"Talk to me, Ben," she said.

"You don't want to hear the words that come from my mouth . . . my gutter mouth," I said, feeling a profound satisfaction at being able to throw that term back at her.

Her face took on that rigid expression she used with such success in business, child rearing, and our marriage.

"You see?" I said with a smile, "all I have to do is remind you of the way I talk sometimes and it makes you mad. But tell me something, Moan. When your lover tells you to suck his cock, do

71

you tell him that he can't use that language on you or do you get all soft and wet and call him 'baby doll'?"

"I don't know why you want to talk to me like this," she said. "I don't deserve it, and I have no lovers."

"No?"

I glanced at her vanity in the corner. There, right out on top, was the little leather satchel. I walked over to it. The abruptness of my movement made her jump backward. I took two steps toward the bag, opened it up, and brought out the package of condoms.

"What's this?" I asked her, holding the box in an open palm.

The look on Mona's face reminded me of why I married her. It was a look both calculating and transparent. She saw that she was caught in a lie and a tryst. But a box of condoms, she reasoned, visibly, was certainly no conviction.

"I haven't used them," she said.

"Come on, Moan, don't be like that now," I was talking in a way that I had so long ago that I hardly remembered. "That man been in your pussy like a gopher down his own hole."

I said it perfectly, even curled my upper lip in a disparaging sneer.

"You bastard," she said.

"Then stand out of the way and let me leave."

Mona saw through the ploy. She realized that I had used words to anger her enough to let me go. But did she also know that I wanted her to see through me, that I wanted to find out what she was up to with Harvard Rollins and his looking into my past.

"I'm not going to let you bait me, Ben," she said. "I want to know what's going on with you, why you're acting so strange."

"Me? You're the one who went to your mother's and didn't even call. And she's not sick either. I doubt if she's even in town."

72

Again Mona needed time to regroup her defenses. She didn't know how much I knew. I had the key to her mom's place. I could have come by. I knew about the condoms. I at least suspected Harvard Rollins of being her lover.

I let her stew in these fears for a moment and then said, "Why don't we go in the living room and talk this out like adults?"

She sat on the sofa and I on my chair. She held her legs at a slant, knees together. I sat spread-legged, hands out to the side.

"What?" Mona asked, her eyes moist, her voice taut.

"I've only had one lover since we've been together," I said, speaking lightly, feeling the liberation of truth. "I know you've had at least three, the last of which is this Rollins guy. I don't blame you. I can only hope that on the off chance that we make love, that you have made sure he's . . . healthy."

Mona was frozen. Her eyes did not know me. The way I was sitting, the words I spoke; I was another man for her—the way I was, but not who I was, for Svetlana. If she would have spoken honestly at that moment, Mona would have said that I had never paid such close attention to her. She would have said that she felt stripped naked and that she didn't like it—not one bit.

"So you admit having a lover?" she said finally.

"Come on, Mona. I won't use the words but you've been doing it too. You've been doing it a lot. And I don't blame you."

"You don't?"

"Baby, listen to me," I said, my own words in my ear. "For years, all the years that you've known me, I've been like a cold-water fish at the bottom of the lake. I haven't done a thing for you except to give you Seela. I don't know how to fuck—excuse me, how to make love. My job is more boring than fungus growing in the dark. I know. You haven't said anything and I just went on.

73

And so now it's out. You got a man who makes you want to carry condoms around in your bag. And me . . . I just need to get back into therapy and figure out what it is that made me into such a, such a blank space."

Every word I said rang true and clear but it was all a cover for what I really wanted from my just-now-estranged wife.

"You don't care if I have a lover?" she asked.

"I care, babe," I said. "It's just that I understand why you would need one. Your life is filled with excitement and sexy people. I've done the same thing every day almost without exception for twenty-two years."

It's odd being so hyperaware of your own words and intentions. I *had* lived an extraordinarily humdrum life. I ate the same kind of doughnut—chocolate, chocolate glaze—every day for twelve years. Then I switched to strawberry yogurt. I loved my job but it was as dry as sawdust, as plain as brown wrapping paper. Mona would be better off with some arty guy with less security and more character.

But all that was over now. I wasn't the same man I had been. Mona was as good as gone. But I needed to know what she was talking about in that bed with Harvard. I needed to know what they knew about me.

"Are you leaving me?" Mona asked.

"I'm gonna move out for a while," I said. "Maybe we'll get back together, but I can't see why you'd want to. I mean, I'm just a lump—that's all I'm ever gonna be."

"What's going on with you, Ben?" Mona asked.

I could tell by her voice that she had accepted my lover and was admitting to her own affairs. She didn't argue about Harvard. She wasn't going to try to keep me home.

74

I felt a twinge of jealousy, realizing that she'd run out of the house tonight to be in her new lover's arms. But I had no time to worry about that. There was something else happening, something more important than all the last twenty-plus years of gray days and lightless nights.

"That's what I wanted to ask you, Mona."

"What, what do you mean?"

"Am I in some kind of trouble, baby?"

"Trouble? What kind of trouble?"

"Why didn't you come home?" I asked simply. "I mean, if you just wanted to be with a lover, you could have met him in the daytime or pretended to be at some event at night."

"My mother—"

"No, honey. Your mother's not sick and we both know it. You were afraid of something, afraid of me."

"The way you, the way you made love to me," she said.

"No. That's not it. You were upset about . . . me. You asked me to go to therapy, you joked about divorce . . . Are you afraid of me? Is there something you're not telling me?"

"No," she said, shaking her head the way she always did when she was hiding something.

I knew then that I wouldn't get any more out of her. She wouldn't break down. The only thing I could hope for was that she was looking for ammunition in the divorce.

She was looking down while I peered over her head at Queens.

Then the phone rang and I got up to answer.

"Hello," I said, remembering Sergei.

"Hey, bro, what you know?"

"Hey, Cass. What's happenin', man?"

"You, my brother, you."

"What's up?"

"We got to have some words, man," the security expert said.

"When?"

"Meet me at the Steak House at five. We don't need a reservation there."

I hung up and turned to Mona.

"I gotta go, honey," I said. "I'll call you later."

"We aren't finished talking."

"For now we are," I said. "Call your boyfriend. Talk to him."

She took a deep breath with which she intended to deny my accusation. But looking into my face she saw that it was useless. Her body went slack on the couch. I got my bag and went toward the door.

"Ben," she called at my back.

"Yeah?"

"Dr. Shriver called. He said that he has an opening tomorrow morning at seven fifteen."

I went out the door, closing it softly as I left.

The Steak House at Park and Forty-sixth was owned by one of Cassius Copeland's old friends from the intelligence branch of the military police. As long as Cassius ate at the bar, he didn't have to pay for food or wine. And so I was waiting there after checking into the Reynard for a two-week stay.

I had a lot of money in the bank, well over a hundred thousand dollars. I never spent anything, and when Mona took vacations, she liked to stay home because she traveled so much for her job. I could pay for the Reynard *and* first-class airfare to any destination in the world.

Sitting at the bar I thought that Hong Kong would be a good place to lose myself, or maybe Ghana. I could pack up and be gone before Mona knew what had happened. Cass would help me. He'd been a captain in military intelligence. He'd told me many stories about ways that men could disappear.

"Hey, bro," he said from behind me.

"Cass, we got to stop meeting like this, man."

"You the only Negro I ever met gets to the appointment before me," he said.

I looked at the clock above the bar; it read 4:46.

"Yeah. I got a lotta time on my hands," I said.

Cassius's expression turned sour. He took a seat on the stool next to me.

"Yeah. Uh-huh. That's why we got to talk."

"Mr. Copeland," a very big white man bellowed from the other end of the bar.

"Joey," Cassius replied.

Joey Bondhauser, owner of the Steak House and half a dozen other popular restaurants, was taller than most men and fatter than anyone I had ever known personally. His blue suit was perfectly tailored, however, and his hands and voice gave the impression of great strength.

Joseph Bondhauser had been a senior communications officer for Army Intelligence in western Europe. Though Cass never told me anything particular about his one-time boss, he implied that all Joey had to do was frown and a man could die anywhere in the world.

"This is my friend Ben Dibbuk, Joey."

"Pleased to meet you," the big man said.

I'd seen Bondhauser before but we had never been introduced.

77

His handshake was powerful. I had the feeling he could have snapped my bones if he wanted to.

"Ben and I got a little business so I brought him here."

"Why don't you take a table in back?" the restaurateur asked.

"Using my Joey-get-a-steak-free card," Cass said with a smile.

"Aw, don't be like that, Cassius," Joey said. "You were one'a my best men. Somebody I could trust. Magda. Magda, come over here."

A very attractive brunette wearing the sheerest of blue gowns came over to us. She was twenty-five, no older and, upon closer examination, quite beautiful.

"Yes, Mr. Bondhauser?"

"You know my friend Cass."

"Yes, sir."

"Give him my private dining room. Everything on the house."

"Yes, sir," she said.

I could see the awe and appreciation in Magda's eyes. She beheld in Joey's huge form power and potential in whose wake she was happily drawn.

"Cass, you ready to take a real job somewhere?" Joey asked then.

"I gotta job, man."

"That make-believe, antiterrorist bullshit?"

"Everything's make-believe, Colonel," Cassius Copeland said. "Nothin's for real."

Deep pleasure infused the fat man's face. He nodded and beamed at my friend.

"You are a dangerous man, Cassius Copeland. You see the truth before anyone else. Magda."

"Yes, sir?"

"Give him everything he wants."

"As you say."

"See you later, Cass," Joey said, shaking the security officer's hand. "Nice meeting you, Ben."

Watching him walk away from us, I was thinking about the words *As you say*. They seemed to imbue the restaurant owner with great power. It struck me as odd that the one obeying was also the person who articulated the degree of Joey's influence. This seemed very important to me at the time.

Magda led us through the dining room and up a slender flight of dark-wood stairs. On the second floor there was a long, narrow hallway that had doors on either side in staggered fashion, so that first there would be a door on the right and then a few paces later there'd be one on the left. At the end of the hall was a double door hewn from solid oak.

Magda took out a key and unlocked the left-hand side. She pushed this open and ushered us in.

The light came on automatically as we entered. There was a large round table attended by four wooden chairs with red velvet seat cushions.

"I'll send up Felix with your menus," Magda said when we were seated.

"I want you to take our orders," Cass said, "but don't bring up anything for fifteen minutes."

Magda smiled and nodded. If the hostess resented the request, she did not show it. She left without another word.

After she was gone, Cass sat back in his chair and stared at me. He did this long enough for me to start to feel uncomfortable.

"What?" I asked at last.

"We got to talk," he said. "But first I'll tell you something about me, something that no one in my everyday life, my real life, knows."

This sudden honesty made me anxious. One of the things about our relationship was that we never talked about our lives at all. Everything was light, impersonal, noncontroversial. I had known for some time that I was probably Cass's only confidant at Our Bank, but even there he was never very forthcoming.

"I'm a man, right?" Cass asked.

"Yes."

"Don't be worried, Ben. Ain't nuthin' wrong here. I'm just tellin' you that when people look at me, they see somethin'. I'm big and strong, tough-minded, and the kinda guy who likes sports. Right?"

"Yeah. I guess that's why I always wondered why you ever even talked to me. I mean, I don't know the first thing about any sport."

"Yeah," he said. "You don't know a baseball from a hockey puck."

We both laughed, though I'm sure neither one of us felt the least bit happy.

"When you told me about the magazines your wife worked on, I went out an' bought some," he continued. "I read her articles. Damn, I read the whole magazines.

"Those are the kind of publications that call a faggot a homo-sexual, right?"

I had never heard Cass use either word. It seemed odd that he used them then, but I nodded, admitting the truth to his claim.

"My friends, Joey and a hundred like him, say faggot. They laugh at 'em. Some of 'em might kick one's ass if he's in the wrong place at the wrong time."

I was lost by now. What could any of this have to do with me?

"You see, Ben," Cass said then. "The one thing, the only thing, I never tell anybody is that I'm a faggot too."

I stared at my work friend of five years, feeling blunted and senseless. I shook my head and crinkled my nose.

"I ain't a girly man," Cass said. "I don't wash the dishes or want a relationship. I'm a man's man, a real man. I fight and fart and wear clothes until they fall apart. Everything about me is man. Everything."

"But what about Joany Winters?" I asked.

It was rumored that there had been a passionate affair between Winters, who was married, and Cassius during his first two years on the job. Secretaries gossiped about how Cass would go into her office for an hour at a time and that she would come out with her hair a mess and her clothes all rumpled.

"I fucked that woman so hard that she had to have two abortions," he said. "There wasn't no way she could explain a black baby to her English hubby."

"But you say you're gay."

"No. I said I'm a faggot. It's your wife's magazines use 'gay' and 'homosexual.' Whenever I get anyplace, I find a girl like Joany and do her for a while. I don't mind havin' sex with a woman; it's just that's not my deepest thing. If you come into a place like Our Bank and get that pussy right off, ain't nobody gonna question you after that. They just see you talkin' to a woman and they know you gettin' somethin'."

I had too many problems on my mind to worry about Cass's sexuality. I don't know if I would have worried about it anyway. What did I care?

"I know this don't mean nuthin' to you, Ben," Cass said, as if he were reading my thoughts. "That's why I'm friends with you. I know that if you knew all about me that it wouldn't make you no nevermind. You don't care. You don't care about nuthin'. That's what I like about you."

"Okay," I said. "You're right. But why are you telling me this after five years? Does it matter?"

"A man named Harvard Rollins came to my office this morning," Cass said, and I went cold. "He told me that he had information about you and that his magazine was doing an article based on this information. He didn't want to embarrass the bank and so he was giving me the chance to help him and limit the effect on the company."

"What did he want to know?"

"Did we have any information about any criminal investigation against you? And if we didn't, could we help his magazine, *Diablerie*, I think, in asking for Colorado records."

"Did he say why they were doing this or what they were looking for?" I spoke deliberately, softly.

"He wouldn't tell me, not exactly, but he did say that it was a crime that they were looking into, a serious felony, he said."

I sat back in my chair thinking about Mona, about her asking Harvard Rollins what he was going to do about me. She wouldn't even tell me. After all those years of marriage she wouldn't even warn me about some chance that I'd be arrested.

"Did you rob a bank or kill somebody?" Cass asked.

"No."

"What did you do?"

"I don't know. I mean . . . when I lived in Colorado, I was a drinker. Every night I did in a bottle of something—whiskey, brandy, gin. A lot of those nights I just don't remember."

"You'd black out?"

I nodded.

"And you wouldn't remember a thing?"

"Sometimes I did. Most times I'd have a general notion of where I'd been, but people would still tell me things that I had no recollection of whatsoever."

"Shit," Cass Copeland said. "Well, you didn't rob any bank during a blackout. How about cars? Did you ever get into a fight when you were drunk?"

"A couple of times I showed up at home beat-up or bruised with some cuts, but I don't remember anything serious. Except one."

"What was that?"

"I ran off the road once. I was drunk."

"That doesn't seem newsworthy," my friend said.

Cass sat across from me, staring into my eyes, shaking his head.

"How long ago did you leave Colorado?"

"Twenty-four years."

"And you've never been back?"

"No."

"Then why all of a sudden would they get on you?"

I stared into Cassius's eyes, wondering if I should share what I knew with him.

"Ben," he said. "The reason I told you about me was because I wanted to tell you that you could trust me. If it got out what I was, if my family ever heard about it, I'd have to kill myself. My father used to tell us boys when we were children that if he ever found out that we was that way he'd kill us with his own hands."

I believed him. I didn't think that he was plotting against me. After the passage of an extremely long minute, I told him what Barbara "Star" Knowland had said to me at the *Diablerie* party.

"Listen, Ben," he said. "If it's just this witness, we could do something about that."

"Huh? What?"

Cass just stared at me, the look on his face as blank as death.

"I need to think about this, man," I said. "I appreciate what you're saying. And you know I would never betray your confidence. But you can see how confused I am. I don't even know what it is I'm being blamed for."

"Yeah. Yeah, I know. It's when you don't know what's comin' you get the most worried. But hear me, Ben, whatever this is I will try and help you. I'ma string this Rollins guy along for a while and act like I'm his friend."

"Thanks," I said. "Listen, I'm not hungry. I'm going to head out."

Cass held out his hand to me. It felt like a lifeline, maybe my only chance for safety. I didn't want to let go. He waited patiently until I had the courage to stand up and walk out of there.

"Hello?" Lana said later that night when I called.

"Hi, baby. I'm just calling to say that I'm not gonna make it tonight."

"You are home?"

"Naw. At a hotel. I just need a night alone."

"I could come and visit for a while," she suggested.

"No," I said. "I'm just gonna lay up here and watch some pay-per-view movies and try to get some sleep."

"Are you mad about something?"

"No. Not at all. But you know I'm going through a lot of stuff right now. I'm trying to figure it all out."

"If you leave her," Svetlana asked, "will you come to me?"

How could I tell Svetlana where I might go tomorrow? I had no idea where'd I'd been or if maybe I'd be in prison later. But she read something else into the silence.

"Please talk to me, Ben, darling."

"Don't worry, Lana. I'll take care of you. I promise."

"Is that what you think I want?" she said, suddenly angry. "You think I am worried about your money? I know men who have much more than you who want me, who tell me that they will give me anything I want."

"It's not that, honey," I said.

But she hung up on me.

I didn't have the strength to call back.

There was nothing I could do. Mona had betrayed me many times over. I didn't mind that she had a lover—but to turn me over to his criminal investigation? And he wasn't even law enforcement, just an investigator for a sensationalist rag.

Why would Mona betray me? But then I thought, why not? I was like an old doorway in her life, something she passed through each day. But I just served a purpose; a barrier against the wind, a surface upon which some suitor might knock. Nothing I said had made Mona laugh in years. I was there to help take care of our daughter and, less and less, someone to go through the motions of physical love with. I brought home a paycheck when she was between jobs, but she never laughed or came or needed me to help her understand a thing.

I watched a children's movie on the hotel pay-per-view system. It was about a young sorcerer with a past he could only guess at. At the end of the film, when he was still in the dark about himself, I became teary.

While the credits were rolling, the phone rang.

It had to be maintenance or maybe the turndown service wondering about the DO NOT DISTURB sign I had hung on the doorknob. No one outside the hotel knew I was at the Reynard. I'd used cash to pay the two-week bill upfront.

"Hello?"

"Can I come up?" Svetlana asked.

"How did you know I was here?"

"Star sixty-nine."

She entered my room all in a rush. She hugged me and kissed me, stared into my eyes as if she were looking for some sign across a vast twilight terrain.

"What's wrong, Lana? Why are you here?"

"Don't you want me anymore, Ben?" she asked.

"Yeah, sure. But I just needed to be alone, to think."

"I wanted to talk to you," she said.

"About what?"

"Sit."

Svetlana was wearing a tiny black dress, no hose and no jewelry. She didn't have any makeup on either. There was something vulnerable about her and the fact that this was probably a calculated vulnerability made her seem all the more defenseless.

She sat next to me and put her hands against my chest. I wondered if she wanted me to kiss her. It didn't seem so. Lana was looking for something, for a way to stop me from moving on, moving away.

"I'm here, honey," I said.

She put her strong arms around my neck and squeezed with all her might. It was a painful embrace. I would have tried to push her off but she was crying. Her faded perfume was a scent that was musky and not at all sweet. I remembered the first time that I met her when she was waitressing at Bulfinch's Café-Restaurant. It was this scent that opened my nose and made me talk to her.

"I told Sergei not to call me anymore," she said, her voice muffled against my chest.

"What?"

She leaned back, still holding my neck with her powerful fingers.

"For a long time you were telling me that you were going to leave me," she said.

"I never said that."

"You said that you expected me to go," she retorted. "Is that what a man says who wants a woman? You would come to see me in the daytime mostly and if I ever said I was busy, you would never complain. It was like you just needed a pretty girl to be on your arm sometimes, or a whore to help you relax because your wife was not so interesting."

"I never said any of that."

"But now, when you finally look at me, Sergei calls and you tell me you cannot see me."

"Who is Sergei?"

"Why didn't you call me back after I hung up on you?"

"I don't know, Lana. I got a lot on my mind. I made you mad once . . . I figured anything I said after that would just make you angrier."

"Because you are mad about Sergei."

"I don't even know who he is."

The words finally got through to her. She was so passionate, so sure of why I was doing what I was doing, that she had miscalculated. She came to tell me that her lover didn't matter when I had only the mildest of suspicions about the rude Russian on the telephone.

I didn't want to duel with the young grad student. I didn't know what I felt. Everyone except maybe Cass had betrayed me. And in turn I had let down everyone I knew. I didn't want revenge. I didn't want to be angry.

"I never made love to him without condom," she said. "And I never let him kiss my pussy or put his thing in my mouth."

Her gray eyes were not quite human to me at that moment. Her blunt honesty made me want to smile.

"Sometimes you wouldn't see me for two weeks," she said, reading her own guilt into my silence.

"And you needed company," I said. "You're a pretty young woman. Beautiful."

"Don't throw me away, Ben. I told Sergei that I wouldn't see him anymore. I mean it."

"But why?" I asked. "Why wouldn't you want a young man who speaks your language and wants to be with you?"

"Why do you say these things to me?" she cried. "Don't you want me?"

For the moment I had the glimmering memory of another woman crying somewhere, another woman asking me for something I didn't understand.

"I did not love Sergei," she said. "He was just there and he wanted to see me."

"The night you called me and said that you were from my job," I said. "Was that because Sergei wouldn't come to you? Were you using me to make him jealous?"

The gray eyes turned suddenly human. Svetlana jumped to her

feet and ran for the door. I let her go. I didn't want her to leave but I let her go. I hadn't meant to vex her with my question. I was just trying to understand—no, nothing so deep as understanding; I just wanted to imagine a world outside my mind.

The door slammed behind her. Now Lana was gone from my life too. At least she didn't know anything about Barbara Knowland. At least she couldn't betray me to Harvard Rollins.

I didn't see Lana being with Sergei as unfaithfulness. She was young and smiling and I paid the rent. I might have done it without the sex.

~

I had been going to Bulfinch's for a few months, mostly for the chance that I could have a brief chat with the Russian girl. One day she was telling me about how hard she worked.

"I work seven days to pay for everything," she said. "I work so hard that I can only take one class a semester."

I asked her how much it all cost. It wasn't much, less by far than Seela's tuition and room and board were at NYU.

"I could pay for that," I said, realizing that it was an offer as it came out of my mouth. "And if you become a big-time international businesswoman, you could pay me back."

It wasn't until the second month of my paying the bills that she had me over for dinner. It wasn't until the third dinner that we went to bed.

It seemed somehow inevitable that we became lovers. It was like a shared responsibility. I never believed that she wanted me. Somehow I thought that all Russians looked down on black people. I don't know where I got that from.

But, I felt, Lana was trapped. She needed someone to take care of her. And if a man foots the bills, then she had to play footsy with him.

~

There came a knock on the door. Svetlana rushed into my arms again. This time we kissed. I could taste the salty tears on her tongue. This excited me. I threw her on the bed and slapped her when she tried to rise. Then I was on her. Then she was on me.

The love we made was oceanic. She was feeling adrift from me and I was like a man dropped in the middle of an unending sea.

"I need you," we said together, laughing at our synchronicity.

"You need me?" we asked together, this time feeling more.

"You are the first man ever to care about me," she said.

"Come on now, Lana," I said, "Woman like you? I bet they line up just to say hi."

"No. I mean, yes. They line up but not because they care. You paid for me and I had to beg you to come to my house. I wore skimpy little dresses and no underwear but you did not try to take me. It wasn't until I took off my clothes that you made love to me.

"You didn't want my body and you didn't want to see my grades or even to see papers that said I was enrolled in school. I just told you that I was needing and you helped me. I have always loved you since then.

"Many men want to fuck me. Many men want me to put on a nice dress and make other men want to fuck me. My teachers want to fuck me and for me to make them look good with my grades and my many languages. I don't mind. I do the work. I fuck them sometimes. But it is always trading a salami for some cheese, a loaf of bread for wine. I live like this and I don't mind. I give my mother money. I will send for my brothers one day.

"But when I meet you, you just say, 'I will pay for that,' and that's all. I have to love you. I have no other choice."

These declarations were simple and straightforward, like her. That's what I had always liked about Lana. Even at the restaurant she was always honest, uncomplicated. It was so much different than with Mona or my parents.

"I did something a long time ago," I said. "Before you were born, I think."

"What?"

"I'm not sure. It was a bad thing, but I don't remember."

"How do you know then?"

"It's been coming up lately. There's a woman who knew me back then who says that we did something, but she didn't say what."

"Did you ask her?"

"I didn't remember her," I said. "I thought that she was mistaken or just mad about me messin' around with her."

"But now you think that she knows something?" Svetlana asked.

"I don't know. But I feel different. I feel like you say, like a new man."

"But you don't like this," she suggested, and then she kissed me.

"I don't know what I did."

"Come," Lana said.

She took me by the hand and led me to the bathroom.

"Stand in the tub," she told me.

I was already naked. She turned on the water and began to soap my thighs. She scrubbed and washed me from head to toe using a

91

glass to rinse off the lather with warm water. She dried me with the plush red towels the Reynard used, and then she took me to the bed and massaged me—for hours. Whenever I tried to speak, she shushed me. Whenever I tried to turn over, she pushed me back on my stomach. Her hands were strong and seemed to get stronger as the night went on. At some point I lost consciousness. It didn't feel like falling asleep but more like tumbling down a dark, dark hole.

I awoke to the sounds of a man yelling and then something both hard and soft, something that made me sick. I sat up in bed gasping. The sounds gripped my heart and pummeled my lungs. For a while I didn't realize that it had been a dream, a sleeping vision.

Svetlana was lying next to me, naked and uncovered. I watched her for a while and calmed down. Age was creeping up on me; life was passing by as if through the window of a car in the country somewhere. All of a sudden there's a beautiful young woman lying on a bench at the side of the road. You see her and slow down. You approach her but wonder what you would do here by the roadside with a beauty who is there for you and unashamed. And then, once you decide that she has more to offer than you can take, you look back at the car and think about the monotonous road ahead of you . . .

These were my thoughts on that morning. It was all very poetic. It was also true. I could stay with Svetlana or go back to Our Bank. I could ask Cassius to ask Joey (or someone like Joey) to kill Barbara Knowland so that my life could begin again with Mona or Lana.

"How are you?" the Russian girl asked.

"Wondering."

"About what?"

"If maybe the idea of suicide is not a good one for a
me."

Lana sat up and put her arms around me. That was wha
wanted. But why hadn't I just asked her to hold me?

Dr. Shriver's office was at the very end of East Fifty-fourth Street.
His second-floor window looked out on the East River, just like
my window did. But his view seemed more intimate.

"Hello, Mr. Dibbuk," the rangy white man said. He was my age
with graying blond hair and the perpetual hint of a smile on his lips.
"How have you been?"

I took the seat across from him, the one that looked out over the
river. There was a lone tugboat out there, 90 percent engine and
10 percent boat.

"All that power and nothing to do," I said.

Shriver's face framed a question that he did not utter.

All around his office were placed and hung African images:
masks, paintings, photographs, and jewelry. When I had first
come to his office, he tried to engage me about African
culture. He knew Africa quite well, had been there a dozen
times. But he soon realized that I knew nothing about that
continent, that dark unconsciousness of a hundred million
displaced descendants of slaves. I didn't know and I didn'
want to know.

"The tugboat," I said. "It doesn't have anything to pu'

"Does that mean something to you?" Shriver asked.

I remembered then that I disliked the analyst's smir' always
felt as if he was making fun of me.

the other

"I ran into a woman at a party my wife took n-five years
night," I said. "She remembered me from nearly

.d that we had done something, implied that it was
.hing illegal. I told her to get away from me."

"Did you know her?"

"She knew my name. I guess she could have asked someone
that, but it didn't seem like a setup. It seemed like she really
remembered me."

"And do you know what she was talking about?" Shriver asked.

"No."

"Not at all?"

I shook my head.

"What were you like twenty-five years ago?" he asked.

This was what he'd always wanted, I thought: to get me to talk
about the earlier years of my life. I had gotten great satisfaction out
of stymieing him, keeping my past secret. It struck me then as a
petty contentment.

"I was a drunk," I said. "When the sun shined I did day work in
construction or some other manual labor. At night I'd drink long
and hard. I'd pick up women or pick fights and wake up with a
headache either way."

"And you don't remember this woman at all?"

"No, sir."

" 'Sir'? Why call me 'sir'?"

"But she thinks that I did something and I think she told the
ple at *Diablerie*."

"*Diablerie*?"

a new magazine that my wife's working for. They say
the playing to the upscale market but they're really just a
sensa list rag."

"A hat does your wife have to say about this?" Shriver
asked, rtable in this world of seeming paranoia.

94

"She hasn't said a thing."

"Then how do you know that this woman . . ."

"Barbara Knowland."

"The one they arrested for those serial killings?" Even Shriver was surprised by this.

"Yeah," I said, and then I launched into the story of how I ended up on the other side of the closet door while Mona tasted Harvard Rollins's dick.

"You were actually in the closet watching this?" Shriver asked, wondering, I could tell, whether to believe me or not.

I nodded.

"How did this make you feel?"

"I don't know. I was surprised that she liked his nasty talk. She never liked it with me."

These last words perplexed the good doctor. He stared at me, as isolated from my mind's inner workings as he had been when I was trying to keep him out.

"Don't you feel betrayed?"

"Yes," I said. "By her knowing that Harvard Rollins is checking up on some crime that Barbara Knowland is blaming me for."

"What about her sexual betrayal?" Shriver asked, more for his benefit than mine, I felt.

"I don't know. I think it bothers me, somewhere deep inside. But you know, I have a way of making feelings go away."

"How do you do that?"

I felt foolish talking about the void living in the hollows of my shoulders, but there was really no other way for me to describe it. It felt good to see the intensity with which the doctor li explanations.

"But none of that matters," I said after finishing up the metaphorical description of my psyche. "What I really want to know is what Star thinks I did all those years ago."

"Why didn't you ask her?"

"I didn't think it mattered until Rollins started looking into my past."

"How can you be sure that he's even doing that?"

"I got that from a friend but I can't say who."

Again the doctor was silenced.

Finally he said, "Why don't we get you to lie down on the couch, Mr. Dibbuk?"

"What for?"

"In classic psychoanalysis the patient lies down and closes their eyes. From this position it is felt that there is a readier access to the unconscious."

"Just relax, Mr. Dibbuk," Dr. Adrian Shriver said to me.

I was on my back on a brown backless couch he had against the wall opposite his window. My eyes were closed and my hands were at my side.

"Okay," I said. "I'm pretty relaxed."

"Tell me about your days in Colorado."

"It's like I said. I was a hard-drinking, hard-loving, hardworkin' young man. Sometimes I'd drink so much that I'd lose whole days, not remember anything I said or did. I had friends but I wasn't close to anybody. I used to make calls back home in my blackouts and blame my parents for all kinds of things."

"What kind of things?"

"I don't know. I don't remember."

"Tell me about a day that you do remember," Shriver said.

This question intrigued me. There was a day in my mind, a day that captured the feeling of Colorado for me.

~

I woke up early on a Sunday morning. The bed smelled of a woman—her perfume and bodily scents. I turned over but there was no one next to me. I went to an open window and gazed out on silvery green leaves shivering in the breeze and filtering the morning sun. I was naked and the house was completely unfamiliar.

The bedroom was on the second floor and the house was set in the woods, on a mountain. There were no neighbors. Outside there was a corral with four beautiful chestnut horses exulting in the wind.

On the bureau was a note.

B,

Thank you for saving me and for such a lovely evening and the ride home. It was wonderful meeting you. I'm off to church now. Maybe we'll see each other again sometime.

H

I supposed that I was B and that H was some woman I had met in a bar. I didn't remember any of it. There was a picture of a young couple on the bureau; a straw-blonde and a ruddy-cowboy kind of guy. I wondered if she was Helen or Henrietta or Holly.

My car was parked on a graded dirt path that passed in front of the big house. I drove for miles trying to find my way back to some kind of city, or at least a paved road. There were, there always were, two quart bottles of whiskey in the trunk of my car. And so when the sun went down and I ran low on gas, I popped the trunk and pulled out the booze.

My memory after that gets a little fuzzy. Some of what I remember might be a dream or a nightmare. I was drinking in the woods, singing to myself and moving between the darkness of pine shadows and the thrilling luminosity of the three-quarter moon. I got lost out there and then some men who were also rambling in the dark saw me and cursed me. They chased me but I was fueled by eighty-six proof.

They split up and I pressed myself into a depression on a rocky hillside.

That was all I had ever remembered before and it wasn't often that I thought about it. But that day on the analyst's couch I saw myself in the moon-cast shadow of stone with a pear-sized rock in my hand. A man passed in front of me. He had a gun, a pistol, and he was searching for me. I leaped out from my hiding place just when he was beyond me. I hit him with more strength than I had ever known. The hardness of his skull, the softness of the tissue underneath, was a familiar feeling . . .

∾

When I opened my eyes, I was holding on to Dr. Shriver by his shoulder and his neck. He was trying to stay in control mentally while attempting to push me off too.

"Take it easy, Mr. Dibbuk," he shouted. "Take it easy."

"What?" I asked.

"What are you asking me?" he replied.

"What did I say?"

I let go and sat down on the brown divan.

98

"You were just coming from a woman's house," he said, lolling his neck to work out the kink I had put there. "And then you were drinking in the woods."

"That's all?" I realized that I was rocking back and forth. I tried to stop but could not.

"Yes," Shriver said. "All of a sudden you sat up and grabbed me."

I was panting. My heart felt too large for its cavity. It was as if I had just killed someone in actuality.

"I got to go," I said, standing up quickly.

"Tomorrow then?" Shriver said.

"What?"

"Tomorrow. You should come back every day until we get to the bottom of this, this trauma."

"Trauma? I didn't say a thing about any trauma."

"Something happened to you, Ben," he had not used my first name before then, "something that caused this deep alienation in you. Talking to this woman has brought it out. If you want to find out what that means, you need to be here on this couch. I will make myself available to you every day, weekends too. You're in a very precarious place."

"Aren't you scared?"

"Of what?"

"Didn't I just jump up and grab you by the neck? And here you say we need to get deeper. Shit, man. We get any deeper and I might throw you through that window."

"And if we don't try," he said with gravity, "you might jump out of that window."

"One day," I said. "I'll come one more time and we'll see."

"Same time," Shriver said. He went to the door and opened it for me.

99

In the small vestibule outside sat a startled-looking young woman with black hair and eyes. She watched me fearfully. She'd probably heard me screaming and the doctor shouting to calm me down.

On the street I was still thinking about that morning in the strange house in the Rockies. I was free and no one knew where I was. I called my boss, got his answering machine again, and told him that I had suffered some kind of trauma and that I had to see doctors for a week.

I went to the Metropolitan Museum of Art and wandered around the Asian collection almost alone.

In the late afternoon I ambled over to Lincoln Center and ate in a large Chinese restaurant near there. I ate a lot because I hadn't eaten yet that day. When I finished, it was three. The blissful feeling of anonymity and freedom stayed with me all that time.

Darkness was up ahead, I knew. Death and demolition were my destination, if not my destiny—that is what I felt. But I didn't care. The void in my shoulders protected me from fear. It infused my mind with a feeling of momentary invulnerability. I wondered what Shriver would have thought about that?

"A paranoid defense system," he might have called it, or "delusions of immunity brought on by anxiety anchored in the feeling of profound guilt."

Whatever it was, I was feeling no pain. I recognized that for years I had secretly wanted to be where I was at that moment: free from the commitment to a meaningless marriage; released from the dreary repetition of binary code and the counting of other people's money.

I walked down Broadway slowly, stopping in stores and resting on the occasional bench. I reached Cooper Union's Great Hall at 5:45, just in time to be admitted to the talk I had looked up the day before in the *Village Voice*.

The doors had only recently been opened but the eight-hundred-seat hall was already half full. I took an aisle seat in the far back row on the right side. There I waited peacefully, like a man who had awakened in paradise that morning and who was still stunned by the rapture.

I watched the audience as they filed in. Hundreds of faces and I didn't know one of them. It was reminiscent of my walk every morning from my apartment to work. I took the same route every day, passing thousands of commuting workers, but rarely did I see a face I recognized. I was unknown and I didn't know anyone—like a ghost haunting a city destroyed by deluge or plague and then repopulated by some alien race.

The lights went down at last and a spotlight struck the podium. A plump man in a light bluish suit walked up to the stage. He had white hair that was too long and dark shoes that clashed with the pastel hue of his clothes.

He introduced himself, but I forget the name, and then launched into a self-referential introduction.

This preamble was long and laborious. The speaker was a lawyer who specialized in death row cases. He knew a lot of famous and infamous people and mentioned all their names. He had been involved in many high-profile cases and there were many corrupt and racist prosecutors who had fallen to his legal scythe.

I didn't care about any of that.

He talked about the number of poor people and people of color in prison. He spoke about how the law was anything but equal and fair.

I didn't care about any of that either. I'd been a black man in America for five decades, almost, and nothing about that meant anything to me. Life for all Americans, whether they knew it or not, was like playing blackjack against the house—sooner or later you were going to lose.

The winners were my bosses' bosses' bosses. They lived in the Alps or Palm Springs or somewhere else where the world is run from.

Black people in prison, Iraqis blown up on job lines in Baghdad, or Vietnamese peasants in their rice paddies becoming target practice for passing American helicopters—we were all dealt a losing hand.

Finally the lawyer got tired of hearing himself crow and so he said, "And now let me introduce the person you've come to hear tonight: Barbara Knowland."

Fifteen hundred and ninety-eight hands came together for Star, the woman wrongly accused of aiding and abetting a serial killer.

With her peacock shawl fluttering behind her, Star ascended the stairs to the podium. She air-kissed the lawyer and stood aside for him to go down into the audience.

Star was carrying a folded square of paper that she placed on the podium. Then she went about moving the microphone down so that it would accommodate her shorter stature. She unfolded the paper, looked at it, looked up, squinting at the spotlight, and then down at the audience.

She took in a quick breath, as if she was about to speak, but no words immediately followed.

"My name is Barbara," she said at last. And everything else was exactly the same as that Sunday night at the launch party for *Diablerie*.

102

I was amazed at her ability to make even this, her own memoir, a tedious and repetitious task, a deadly dull chore without the slightest variation or added nuance.

I listened to her for half an hour, after which I felt that I could make the same presentation if only someone would lend me a peacock shawl.

After it was over, people gathered in the lobby to buy the book and to line up for her signature.

I bought a copy and waited in line.

Both Mona and Harvard Rollins were standing behind Star. This didn't surprise me, as the ad for the reading had said that it was sponsored by *Diablerie*.

The adulterous couple weren't holding hands or touching in any way but you could tell that they were drawn to each other. They weren't looking into the line or they would have seen me.

"Excuse me, sir," a young woman said. She had Elizabeth Taylor eyes and the plainest of plain faces. She was carrying a small block of yellow stickies and a blue felt pen.

"Yes?" I said.

"Do you want your book personalized?"

"Excuse me?"

"Do you want Ms. Knowland to put your name along with her signature?"

"No. No, her name will suffice."

The young white woman found my turn of phrase unsettling. She stared at me and backed away, bumping into the woman behind me in line.

I didn't blame her. There was something off about me, something slightly sinister or even evil. I waited patiently, coming up behind the throng of mostly women—ladies who wanted to touch the woman who had seen and survived the daily, unspoken threat of all women's worlds: malevolent men with sharp knives and manacles who are only here on earth to destroy beauty.

I put my book down when my turn came. Mona noticed me then, but instead of saying something to me, she touched Harvard's shoulder. This gesture would have been heartbreaking if only I had loved her.

The faux detective was turning to see what she wanted when Star Knowland asked, "Do you want me to inscribe your name in the book?"

She hadn't even bothered to look at who stood before her.

"To one of my oldest and dearest friends," I said. "Ben."

Star's head shot up.

"What are you doing here?"

"I thought we should talk, so I came to buy a book and ask you if you'd have coffee with me."

"I thought you didn't want to talk to me."

"I was confused when I saw you. I really didn't remember."

"Do you remember now?"

"Only little pieces," I said. "And most of that might not even be real."

"I'm staying at the Fairweather until Monday," she said haltingly. "Call me . . . and we'll meet someplace." She signed the title page and closed the book, giving me the same stare that the homely woman with the beautiful eyes had.

"Ben," he called as I made my way out the front door of the hall.

It was Harvard Rollins. He caught up quickly and grabbed me by the right biceps.

"Yeah?"

"We need to talk," he said, looking around as if contemplating committing a crime.

"I know everything I need from you," I said.

I tried to move away but he held on to my arm.

"What's that supposed to mean?"

"Mona told me."

"Told you what?" he asked.

"She said we had to break up because you two were lovers now."

"What?"

"Yeah. She said that you were together at her mom's place and that she asked you to wear a condom but you just pushed her down on her knees and fucked her bareback." I smiled. "Then she said that you made her suck on your thing and that she couldn't have unsafe sex with me if she was having it with you too. Now if I want to have sex with her, I have to wear a condom . . . to protect you."

There was just enough truth in what I said to make him question Mona. I liked that. I wanted to fuck with him.

He was bothered by my words but he had an agenda that would not be derailed.

"There's somebody I need you to meet," he said.

"I got an appointment."

Harvard's grip tightened.

"First you have to come with me."

It occurred to me that I wouldn't be able to get away from Rollins. He had been a New York City cop and could certainly subdue me. I thought about trying to sucker punch him but I doubted if I could catch the powerful ex-policeman unawares.

"Hey, you guys," someone said.

It was Cassius Copeland, walking over to our isolated part of the granite stairs.

He came right up to Harvard, a big smile on his dark face, proffering his right hand. Then suddenly, when he was in range, he jutted out with his left. He was holding one of those electronic stunning devices. Harvard saw it coming. He released me and made to lunge at Cass. But the stunner hit him in the diaphragm and then Cass socked him in the jaw with a short but powerful right hook. Before Rollins could fall, Cass caught him around the waist.

"Here, let me help you," Cass said, and he supported the weight of the dazed detective until he was sitting on the ground with his back up against the wall.

"Just wait here, Mr. Rollins," Cass said, "while me and Ben get us all a taxi."

Cass took me by the arm and led me away.

Rollins tried to yell something at us as we departed but the shock had debilitated his capacity for speech.

"You want anything else, Ben?" Cass asked me at a little Italian bistro on Sixth Avenue.

"No thanks."

I had ordered a creamy pasta dish with truffles that went for a hundred dollars a plate and Cass had eighty-year-old cognac. It's amazing what you can get in New York.

"How did you know I'd be there?" I asked the security expert.

"I didn't," he said. "I just Googled Barbara Knowland and saw that your wife's magazine was hosting her reading at Cooper Union."

"So you thought you'd check her out?"

"Sure," he said. "Why not? You know she's staying at the Fairweather, room eight twenty-nine."

"How did you get that?"

"Homeland Security, brother. I got some friends up in there. With just an eight-digit security code you can follow about ten percent of the people in this country at any given moment. Hotel reservations, interstate travel rosters, ATM hits, and credit card purchases."

Cass was beginning to amaze me.

"She could have a heart attack up in there with no problem," he said.

"You'd actually do that for me?"

"Why not?" Cass asked. "You're my friend, right?"

"I need to know more," I said. "I've got to talk to her. She said she'd have coffee with me."

"Don't do that, Ben. Don't meet her anywhere she knows about beforehand."

"Why not?"

"Who was the guy Rollins wanted you to meet?"

"I don't know," I said.

"But it's somebody got to do with this thing Star's talkin' about. You better believe that. You make a meetin' with her and you'll have some serious uninvited guests."

"Yeah," I said. "I guess that's right. But who could it be?"

"Doesn't matter. You okay right now, man. Just keep cool. Let things settle down a little bit. I'll cover you at work. Let me look into this Colorado angle some more and then we'll talk."

Cass paid for the meal and I gave him the number of my hotel.

After that I wandered about until ten or so and then returned to my room.

Lana was there. I'd left her my spare key card but for some reason I believed that she wouldn't want to see me again.

"What would you say if you found out that I was a murderer?" I asked her near midnight. We'd made love twice and were touching each other, tentatively considering a third try.

"What kind of murderer?"

"Are there different kinds?"

"Many," she said, the youthful voice of deep experience.

"Like what?"

"There are men who kill for fun or because they are rotten inside and hate everyone. There are men who kill women. There are soldiers who kill in battle and lovers who kill for revenge. Sometimes mothers kill their babies because they do not wish to see them suffer."

"Is it okay sometimes for a killer to get away with his crime?" I asked, feeling as if I were getting expert testimony.

"No one ever gets away," Lana said in a soft, serious voice.

"No?"

"No," she said, and then she kissed me.

My body seemed to surge up out of itself toward her. We made love again. It was a shuddering kind of passion between us. I couldn't ejaculate, I was used up in that way, but I felt something powerful coming from her. It was a feeling both bitter and necessary.

"Ben?"

I came awake trying to remember the last time a lover had aroused me in my bed deep in the night. I smiled thinking about Lana calling my house, pretending to be from work.

"Yeah?"

"I don't care."

"About what?"

"If you have killed somebody. It is all right with me. You are a good man. You are good to me. I love you."

"Take the couch again, Ben," Dr. Shriver said when I moved toward my regular chair.

I was afraid of the backless brown chaise longue by then, haunted by the memory of that rocky cove and the man dying by my hand, the back of his skull crushed to pulp.

"It's okay," Dr. Shriver said. "I'm here with you. We'll go through this together."

I sat and then lay down. When I closed my eyes, I thought that I'd be back in that fantasy or memory or whatever it was.

"Tell me about your father," Shriver said.

A rush of calm went through my fearful mind . . .

⁓

He was a tall man, or at least that's how it seemed to me, with big black hands and serious eyes. He'd always tell me and my brother how easy we had it.

"When I was a child," he'd say, "I didn't go to school past grade five. I didn't think about ice cream or television or hula hoops. There was only one radio on our whole block. We never knew that there was a stock market crash or a depression. We were already as depressed as we could get."

And he really was depressed. At night he would sit in his recliner drinking vodka and smoking cigarettes. To the world he was a happy guy, always ready to smile or tell a joke. People who met my father liked him, were drawn to him; they wanted to spend time with him and share his happiness.

But that face, the one he presented to the world, wasn't our father.

If Briggs or I got him angry by doing something against him or our mother, he'd whip us with his leather strap. He'd make us strip down to our briefs and lie down on a bed while he lashed us.

I remember crying out, "I won't do it again, Daddy!" and him saying, "I know you won't. Not after I finish with you."

What did your mother do when this was happening?

My mother fretted in another room, out of sight of the beatings we got. And later on, when we cried to her, she'd say that it wasn't all that bad. A week later she would even tell us that we were imagining it, that our father never beat us.

Maybe she even believed that lie.

~

I sat up on the couch after half an hour of these laments.

"A lot of fathers beat their kids," I said. "That doesn't mean anything."

Shriver said nothing to this. There was no smirk on his lips to contradict the deep sympathy in his eyes.

"Tomorrow?" he asked. "Same time?"

"Tomorrow's Sunday."

"I'm not doing anything," he said. "So tomorrow?"

It was eight A.M. when I left the therapist's office but the heat was already beginning to rise in the humid air. Across the way was a small concrete plaza that hovered above the river. I went out there and sat on a bench, wondering about the things I'd said on the couch.

A tall and slender white man in black jeans and a checkered shirt came up and sat down on the bench across from me. He lit a cigarette, reminding me of the pack in my pocket.

The act of striking the match for my Camel brought my father full-blooded into my mind.

There was no doubt of the love he felt in his heart for me and my brother. He would have died for either one of us. He'd been a tough man in his Texas youth. Down in Galveston he carried a gun and a razor. One night he laid in wait for a man, whom he stabbed but who, he said, did not die.

My brother and I speculated on the minutiae of my father's confession.

"You know he said that that man lived," Briggs said, "because he don't want us to think that killin's okay."

"But he didn't say that he was tryin' to wound the mothah-fuckah," I argued. "He said he stabbed him and that means he wanted to kill him."

"Nuh-uh," Briggs replied. "No he didn't."

But whether he had or had not intended to kill that man, whether that man had or had not died, didn't matter. The fact remained that our dictator father had attacked a man with a knife. We believed him because he attacked both of us every month with his strap. He showed no mercy, never apologized about these beatings. He wouldn't listen when we'd say that we were good children who deserved better.

"Mr. Dibbuk?" the man in the checkered shirt asked, interrupting my gut-wrenching reverie.

111

I looked up into his pale face, considering the Western twang to his words.

"Are you the guy Harvard Rollins wanted me to meet?"

He smiled and nodded.

"Winston Meeks is my name," he said.

He put out a hand but I did not take it.

"My wife told you about my appointment yesterday too late?" I speculated. "And so you dropped by today on the off chance I'd be here."

"I'm with the Colorado State District Attorney's Office," Meeks said, sitting down next to me on the stone bench. "We'd like to have an interview with you if you don't mind."

"Or maybe you were going to talk to the doctor," I added.

Again, I thanked God for that cigarette, God and my father for showing me how to keep my cool when the world wants to get at me.

"We could file a complaint with the New York state attorney," Meeks said.

I inhaled the tar and nicotine, cyanide and just plain smoke.

"We could ask for you to be extradited," he added.

"Then why haven't you?"

"Because we'd like to hear your side of the story first."

"What story is that?"

"Mr. Dibbuk," Winston Meeks said. "We won't get anywhere with you playing coy. Come with me to my office and we'll talk this out."

"Your office is in Denver, right?"

"I'm using the Plaza Hotel as my base of operations." He stood up, expecting me to stand too. I admit that he had power in his voice. I wanted to go with him but I resisted the urge. I was a small boat tethered to the dock in the face of a great swell.

"This here bench is my base of operations," I said, gripping the seat with the fingers of my left hand. "Why don't you depose me right out here in plain sight?"

Meeks was not used to being refused or contradicted. I wondered how important this cowboy was, back home in Colorado.

Finally he sat, realizing that he couldn't pry me loose.

"Do you know a man named Grant Timmons?" he asked.

"Never heard of him."

Meeks's eyes turned into slits. I believe that if we were in his private office I'd have gotten slapped right then.

"He died two years ago next Thursday."

"That's too bad," I said. "Was he an old man?"

"Fifty-seven."

"Does this have anything to do with me, Mr. Meeks?"

"He was convicted of killing Sean Messier." Meeks was staring daggers at me then.

"Yeah?"

"He died still serving his sentence," Meeks said, "the sentence that Barbara Knowland says that you deserved."

"Say what?"

"When did you leave Colorado, Mr. Dibbuk?"

It was my turn to stand up.

"I don't like this turn of questions, Mr. District Attorney," I said. "For the record, I don't know anyone named Timmons or Messier. Beyond that I don't have to answer your questions and I have no intention of doing so."

"Where can I get in touch with you if I need to?" Meeks said, rising also.

"My house. My apartment."

"Your wife says that you moved out."

"Don't believe everything you hear, Mr. Meeks. Hearsay is a motherfucker."

I went straight to the New York Public Library at Forty-second and Fifth. There I utilized the computer system to access old Denver newspapers. In the *Denver Post* there was an article dated July 1, 1979. A man named Sean Messier was found next to a woodpile that sat at the side of his rural home, his head caved in due to a blow from a hard and heavy object. I found another article from that September that reported Grant Timmons had been arrested for the crime. It said that he was a rival of Mr. Messier for the affections of an unnamed woman and that Timmons could not account for his whereabouts on the night of the murder. Actually, he had lied about where he was and therefore made himself a suspect.

Apparently, Sean had gotten into a fight with Grant a week before. Messier was an accomplished pugilist; he beat up Grant pretty bad. The prosecution speculated that Grant had come up to Messier when he was getting wood for a fire. He hit the un-suspecting Messier with a steel pipe or a crowbar, which he must have discarded elsewhere.

It was enough for a conviction. Grant Timmons, it seems, was a bully of inordinate proportions. He'd been involved in many fights over the years and he always got revenge on those that bested him in anything. He was the perfect suspect in any crime. And here he had actually been in a fight with the victim only a short while before.

There were other articles but no new information.

By September I had already left Denver for New York. I had both of my near-fatal accidents soon after the death of Sean Messier, but that didn't prove anything. Not a thing.

I tried to think if there was any shred of a memory of somebody named Messier in my mind. He was much older than I was. He was a pilot for a small company and a war hero from Vietnam. There was no place that we would have run into each other except maybe some bar somewhere. But what would I have been doing outside next to his woodpile? Why would I have ambushed him there?

It made no sense to me. It didn't sound like me.

I was a drinker, a fighter when I was drunk, but I was no assassin. And even if I had gotten angry enough to kill someone, I should have had some memory of who that someone was.

The Fairweather was uptown on the East Side. It was a small hotel but still large enough to have a restaurant and so I could walk in without being noticed. I was just inside the door when I saw Harvard Rollins coming out from the elevator on the far side of the reception desk. I went up to the concierge and asked for the house phone, not because I wanted to call anyone, but just to avoid another conflict with the magazine detective.

I asked the hotel operator for Sean Messier's room. I don't know why I used that name. Maybe it was a sense of irony or just the fact that that was the name I'd been trying, unsuccessfully, to remember.

When the hotel operator failed to find the person I was looking for, I thanked her and turned around.

I was a part of the scenery by then. I'd used the phone, so it was no surprise to see me taking the elevator. I got out on the eighth floor and knocked on the door numbered 829.

Star certainly was not expecting me. She would have closed the door in my face but I pushed past her.

Her room was what they call a junior suite. Bigger than a regular room, it had enough space for a small settee with a stuffed chair at its side. I sat in the chair and put up my hands, indicating that I just wanted to talk.

"That detective from *Diablerie* is coming," she said, trying to move me out with words. "He wants to turn you over to the Colorado authorities."

"You mean Winston Meeks?" I said.

That stopped Star with her mouth open.

"And Harvard just left your room," I added. "I doubt if he'll be back anytime soon."

"What do you want, Ben?"

"You say my name like you've known it your whole life," I said, "and here I don't even recognize you."

"How can that be, Ben? You and I were together when you killed a man."

I felt a coolness run through my chest like the breeze out of an open tomb.

"I don't remember anything about anything like that," I said, almost absolutely certain of my ignorance.

"Then why did you come to my readings?"

"The *Diablerie* dinner was because my wife made me go," I said. "The college was to get you to tell me why you're doing this to me."

"I'm only protecting myself," she said. "The first time in my life that I do something right and you come out of the woodwork to threaten me with more trouble."

"Miss Knowland," I said. "You have to understand me. I don't want anything from you."

116

"Not now," she said. "Not now that I've told the authorities all that I know. Now if there's a trial, you'll be the one in the docket. You'll be the one to go to prison. I'm not going to pay for what you did."

As she spoke, Barbara Knowland's face distorted into a kind of malleable rage, like that of an infant who does not comprehend her own emotion. She had worried for years about someone like me coming out of the shadows.

"But I don't remember," I said.

"How can I believe that?"

"Why would I kill anyone?" I asked. "What reason would I have?"

"Blind, drunken rage," she said. "We went up to his house together. I just wanted you to help me move my things. It was you who went crazy. He told you to get off of his property and let his guard down. That's when you hit him with your crowbar or whatever."

"If I was such a demon, then why didn't you turn me in to the cops?"

"You know we didn't do things like that back then," she said again, like an old friend. "Things happened and we just moved on."

It was true as far as it went. Drug dealers and burglars, car thieves and gangs were all a part of my social landscape back in my drinking days. I could remember many crimes and criminals that I would have never even considered reporting.

But I had never been with anybody who'd committed murder. At least I didn't remember being there.

Squat and middle-aged, Barbara "Star" Knowland peered into my eyes. She was nervous, scared of me, of what I might do.

I raised my hand to scratch my eyelid and she flinched. This fearful gesture was more damning than her verbal accusation. She was actually afraid of me. Maybe she really had seen my rage before.

I thought about Svetlana sprawled on the floor where I had thrown her.

"Why don't you sit down, Star?"

"I'm fine where I am."

"What did you tell Meeks?" I asked her.

"I told him about Messier," she said, screwing up her courage. "I told him what happened."

"What happened?"

"I, I don't think I should be talking to you about it. If there's a trial, you could use it."

The meanings behind the words that my accuser spoke went through me like waves of electricity. She had seen me, remembered me, called my wife's magazine, called the Denver prosecutor. Because of her I might soon be in prison clothes standing trial for a crime I had no inkling of.

I stood up, feeling the strength in my thighs. I reached out to take Barbara by the arm. She opened her mouth and I said, "Do not yell," and she remained silent as I pulled her toward me.

I witnessed all these events unfolding as if they were the actions of another man.

"What happened that night?" I asked her.

"I can't tell you."

"Listen, bitch," I said. "You came up to me when I didn't know you. You blindsided me and then you turned me over to the cops. You are the only one who knows about this, as far as I can see. And so tell me what you know right now."

There was a threat wrapped up in my words to her. I wondered if I meant it.

"We met in a bar outside of Boulder," she said. "You had been drinking already, and Sean Messier had kicked me out of his house—"

"You were his girlfriend?"

"I was fucking him and he was feeding me. But I got pregnant and he didn't want to pay for an abortion. He drove me down to the highway and put me out on the side of the road. It was two days after that that I met you. We started messing around and I told you about what he'd done. I was hoping that maybe you'd help me with some cash but you said that we should go up to his house and steal enough for the abortion.

"I, I didn't want to rip Sean off, but he did have my things in a trunk, so I said we could go. I knew his flight schedule and so we drove up there after he was gone."

"What do you mean, 'his flight schedule'?"

"He was a small-plane pilot who worked doing deliveries for a farm-supply company."

"Were we drinking?" I asked.

"You had a couple of quarts of whiskey in the trunk. We drank one of the bottles on the way up to his place. You broke through his big picture window in the living room and then I went upstairs to get my trunk and, and the money he kept in a cigar box in his bathroom. It was you who said that we should fuck in the living room. If you hadn't started that shit, we would have been out of there before he got back. If we weren't doin' it, we would have heard him before he dragged you off me and took you outside."

"I thought you said he was working?" I said, squeezing her arm tighter.

119

"He was supposed to be but he came back. It was raining that day . . . I don't know."

"What happened then?"

"I don't know."

"What do you mean, you don't know?"

"You guys went outside. I was afraid to go. I knew how mad Sean could get. You guys went out there and then, maybe five minutes later, you came back and told me that you took care of him."

"I told you that I killed him?"

"You said that you took care of him," she said with real fear in her voice. "I didn't know what to do. You told me that we had to get out of there, but I was afraid to be with you. You told me that you didn't care about me anyway. You put on your clothes, took the money, and left.

"After you drove off, I went to see if I could help, help Sean. But he was dead. The side of his forehead was crushed. So I took his car and drove it to Berkeley, where my sister lived. I told her what had happened and we had the car junked.

"You're hurting me, Ben."

I was gripping her upper arm as hard as I could. I released my hold, thinking of what she had said. I didn't remember any of it— not the woman, not the pilot, not the murder, not anything.

Barbara had fallen into the chair, holding her hurt biceps with her good hand.

"I don't know you," I said.

"How could you forget?" she asked. "You killed him."

"You don't know that," I said, floundering. "You didn't see me do it."

"What else could it have been?"

120

The tone of her question made me look closer at this woman, my nemesis. Her defiance made her brave—not in a heroic way, but the kind of bravery that criminals have. Here I was standing before her, a greater force, and she was threatening my borders. She was afraid of me, but at the same time she wasn't backing down.

I considered killing her; I really did. I tried to imagine my hands around her throat. I thought of her on the floor beneath me, my knees snapping her ribs as I strangled her. The desire was there but it was weak, unable to bring the strength of murder to my fingers.

I stood there staring at her. She rose up and went around me. I think she could see the murder in my eyes.

She went to the door, opened it, and said, "You should go."

Three very dark, French-speaking African men came into the elevator on the second floor. They were wearing business suits and having a serious conversation. I accompanied them out of the hotel and departed their company when they asked the doorman to hail them a taxi.

On the street I wondered about Barbara Knowland's story. Why would she lie about something like that? It made sense, if events occurred the way she related them, that she'd be petrified to see me at her reading. The police had already put her on the hot seat for murder; all I had to do was blame the killing on her. Maybe she thought that I'd come to blackmail her.

"Oh my God! Oh my God! Oh my God!" a woman shouted from one of the apartments in my daughter's new building.

I remember thinking that she'd have to hear her neighbors rutting all the time now that she was living in a building like this. It was the same way when I was a kid in Colorado. But back then I was the one doing the rutting; either that or I was passed out from liquor.

I knocked on her door and the screaming stopped. Even then I only marveled at the thinness of the walls: The lovers could hear me knocking right through my daughter's walls.

"Who is it?" Seela called.

"Me."

The silence that followed was profound. Sixty seconds passed before the door came open. My ugly-duckling daughter was standing there in a ratty blue housecoat next to a chubby white boy who was wrapped in a bright orange robe that was made for a woman. I could see the outline of his waning erection through the thin, tightly held cloth.

"Hi, Daddy," Seela said. "This is Martin. My, um, friend."

"What happened to Jamal?"

"Nothing."

"Oh," I said. "I see. Martin?"

"Yes, sir?"

"Put on some clothes and give me a few minutes with my daughter. You could go down to the coffee place at the corner. She'll be with you in a few minutes."

They had been going at it on a thin mattress in the middle of the living room floor. Martin bent down to pick up his clothes and rushed into the bathroom. I walked over to the mattress and nudged it with my toe.

Seela busied herself at the sink, turning on the water and rinsing something. There wasn't much furniture in the apartment. Seela had brought in a small red table and two blue chairs that she'd bought some years ago on a family vacation to New Hampshire.

122

I sat in one of the blue chairs and Martin came blundering out of the bathroom. The buttons on his shirt weren't lined up straight.

"I'm going to go back to the theater, Seel," he said. "Call me later."

My daughter waved at him, not saying a word.

"What are you doing?" she said in a very loud voice the moment Martin closed the door behind him.

"Came to see my girl," I said with my patented fake smile.

"And why mention Jamal?"

"He's your boyfriend, isn't he?"

"So?"

"So what if Jamal came up here to see you and he hears Martin there fuckin' you so hard that you sound like you're in your own private church?"

Seela had never heard her daddy say anything even remotely like that. Her mouth opened but the words would not come. I believe that she would have cried if she wasn't too much in shock to remember how.

"Baby," I said.

"No. No, no, no, no, no," she said. "Don't you say anything else to me."

I told my daughter that I had heard her fucking and coming through the door. I could have told her that I paid the rent on that door. I could have said that what she did was putting her business all down the hall. But none of that would have been right. I didn't have to pay her rent. She didn't have to respect me, or herself for that matter. I was wrong, but I hadn't meant to hurt her.

While I had these thoughts, Seela began to cry. She was trembling from her diaphragm. Her hands gripped the blue cloth of her housecoat. She wanted to say something but there was nothing to say. My walking into her apartment and not averting my eyes or my words had stripped her bare. This was, I thought, a truly traumatic experience.

"Why, Daddy?" she said at last.

"Sit, baby."

She sat across from me on the other crayon-blue chair. I smiled at her and reached out to touch her wrist.

She shifted her body away from me.

"Honey," I said. "I don't care about what you were doing here . . ."

"Martin's Millie's boyfriend," my daughter said. "She's at the theater working on stage design and he dropped by to pick up some of her plans. He's the one that told Millie that she should share the apartment with me."

"That's okay, baby."

"It's not okay. I betrayed my boyfriend and my roommate."

She was miserable at her perfidy. I could see that she felt I was some kind of divine justice come to damn her.

"It's not so bad," I said.

"How can you say that?"

"You're just a kid," I said. "I mean, I did worse than this almost every day when I was back in Colorado."

"All you did was get drunk a lot," Seela said. "Mommy told me that you drank until you had an accident and then you stopped."

I was little more than a ghost in my daughter's life, an apparition. We'd never talked about anything but money if she needed it, and math, her worst subject in school, when the homework was due.

"I used to have a friend back in those days named TJ," I said, remembering him as I spoke. "He had this beautiful Danish girlfriend named Chara.

"TJ and me used to drink pretty hard. Some nights he was so drunk I had to carry him into his house and put him in the bed for Chara. One time she was so mad that she seduced me and we did it right there in the same bed where he was sleeping."

Seela was looking at me now, into my eyes. With just those few words I could tell that I was no longer the milquetoast daddy that Mona had invented for her.

"You did it while he was right there?" she asked.

"Snoring like a bull walrus."

I smiled.

She snickered.

I laughed.

Seela actually guffawed, showing all her teeth.

"What happened after that?" Seela asked once she'd gotten control of herself.

"I went out drinkin' with TJ every night for two or three weeks."

"*No.*"

"Oh yeah. And I'd pay for all his drinks. Every night Chara would be waiting at the door in her nightie. I'd ask her to go in the other room but she wanted to do it right up next to her boyfriend—either in the same bed, on the floor, or in his favorite stuffed chair."

"Did he ever catch you?"

"One night we were goin' at it in his chair when all of a sudden we heard him say, 'Chara.' He was sitting up in the bed. She said, 'Go back to sleep, baby, me and Ben are just talking.' He slumped back down and we went at it . . . like dogs."

125

I hadn't thought about TJ and Chara since I left Colorado. Remembering them brought Mona and Harvard Yard to mind. I was no better than them. As a matter of fact, I was worse.

"Daddy?" Seela was saying.

"What?"

"I asked you if you ever felt guilty."

"Not then. Not consciously. The night after that I stopped going out drinkin' with TJ. I took a construction job outside Boulder and never saw either of them again."

"Do you feel bad now?"

I looked at the daughter I didn't know and who didn't know me. I opened my mouth but there was nothing to say. The silence that passed between us carried more information than nineteen years of the father-daughter relationship.

"Why'd you come over, Daddy?"

I could have told her that my life was filled with unanswerable questions like that one, that the fabricated structure that kept me going for two decades had fallen apart and now I was floating around like a baby black widow spider wafting on the breeze. I had no reason to be in that apartment, confessing to a youthful betrayal. I was looking for an anchor, and like a fool, I had snagged on to my little girl.

I should have walked out of there but instead I told Seela about the dinner Mona and I went to, about Star and Harvard Rollins and the man named Meeks. I skipped the part about spying on her mother having sex with Rollins, but I told her that I was sure they were having an affair.

"And when you saw Mommy, she turned away to this detective guy?" Seela asked. Martin and Jamal and Millie were the furthest things from her mind.

"Like I said, she's been having an affair with him," I said. "Don't get me wrong, honey. I've had an affair too."

"With who?"

"That doesn't matter right now. You don't know her."

"And did you kill somebody, Daddy?" my plain-faced daughter asked.

"I don't know," I said. "I certainly don't remember killing anyone. I never entertained the idea until this Barbara Knowland came on the scene."

"Maybe she's lying," Seela suggested.

"Why would she make up some elaborate lie like that?"

"Maybe she killed him. Maybe you did go up there with her and drink until you passed out. Then, then maybe this guy came back and she hit him from behind a door with a crowbar, and when you woke up, you left and never even saw him. And now that she sees you sitting in the audience, she's worried that you figured it out and that you'll send her to jail."

Seela transformed in front of me at that moment. For years she had just been there: infant, toddler, child, adolescent. Whatever she was, it was as far away from me as a distant moon in orbit around a dead planet. I had only cared about her as a responsibility, not as a person, and she'd never said one thing that touched me.

But now that was all washed away. Seela had shown me how I might be fooled. Barbara Knowland walked up to me wanting to know why I was there. When I didn't recognize her, she thought that it was an act; she believed that I was going to turn her in for the crime she'd committed decades ago. Maybe I'd heard about her publishing deal and meant to blackmail her.

Of course she would have been the one to kill this Sean Messier, not me. She had the relationship with him. She was pregnant by

127

him. I was no more than a rolling drunk who came to a stop in the wrong place at the wrong time.

I reached out to take my daughter's hands in mine.

"Seela," I said. "You are my savior."

"Daddy, are you all right?"

Someone knocked on the door. The sudden sound made us both gasp and flinch as if we were caught in a moment of criminal intimacy.

Seela stood up and went to the door. She opened it.

"Hi, honey," she said to Jamal.

He was like many of Seela's boyfriends: tall, very dark, and quietly handsome. She liked men and boys in that cast but always felt, her mother had told me, that she was never good enough to keep them.

I stood up and put out my hand to him. We'd met a few times when I brought clothes or books or, more likely, a check to the dorm for Seela.

"Mr. Dibbuk," he said. "How are you, sir?"

"Lucky to have a daughter as wonderful as this child here."

"Yeah, she's great."

I gazed into his dark eyes, wondering if his words were echoed in his heart. Very little I had ever said had meaning in my soul. My true feelings were trussed up in a thousand lies I used to get by. Hence, I never believed anything that anyone told me. This thought came to me like a revelation. I hardly ever believed anything but I did believe Star. I did not question her. Maybe that was because her accusations resonated with the man I buried deep inside me.

"Are you ready?" Jamal was asking Seela.

"For what?"

"To go to Millie's play," he said.

"Oh," Seela uttered. I could see Millie and Martin and her betrayal rising up into her face.

"Go on, baby," I said then. "Get dressed. I'm gonna be okay now that we talked and you are too. We both know what's important."

"Really, Daddy?"

"I'm going home to talk to your mother now."

I don't know what she thought I was saying but the words seemed to give my daughter some relief. She put her arms around my neck and kissed my cheek.

"I love you, Daddy," she said, leaning back and looking into my eyes.

"I love you too," I said. What else could I say?

Mona was on the couch crying when I got home. At first she thought I could have been someone else.

"Who is it?" she whined when I came through the door.

She was desolate on the cushions, crying into the roseate floral pillow. When she looked up at me, I could see that her despair had nothing to do with me.

"He dropped you?" I asked.

She pressed her face back against the pillow.

I sat down next to her and put a hand on her shoulder. She sat up and put her arms around my neck as our daughter had done.

"Ben," she cried.

I wanted to tell her that Rollins would have left her anyway, that she was just a dalliance on a long road of women that the detective was traveling. I wanted to confess about my lies to him, but for some reason—for the first time in a long time—I didn't want her to let me go.

129

"I'm so sorry," she said. "I lost my mind. I wanted somebody to love me. I wanted it so bad. But he, he just told me that it was over, like he was mad. I don't know what I did."

I let her hold on to me, unbothered by her need to lament her lover's abandonment. What did it matter anyway? I hadn't been there for her. I couldn't figure out how to talk to her in the bedroom, at the dinner table, in the morning when there was possibility in the air.

For a long time we sat like that. She molded to my form and bleated.

Many minutes later the phone rang.

"Should I get it?" I whispered.

She nodded.

"What if it's him?"

"I don't want to talk to him," she said, looking up at me.

"Hello?" I answered the phone.

"Ben?" Harvard Rollins said. "What are you doing there?"

"What do you want?"

"Is Mona there?"

"She doesn't want to talk to you."

"I have to speak to her," he said, with some urgency in his voice. "It's important."

"She said that she doesn't want to talk. Maybe you could drop by her office tomorrow. Right now she's on the couch crying her heart out."

"You're a motherfucker, Dibbuk. I could have you arrested for what you did to me last night."

"I didn't do anything to you, Officer Rollins. You just fell on your ass, man."

"Let me speak to Mona."

I hung up then and took a deep breath. I was still as lost as I had been before. But now I felt a little better. All the pieces to the game I was playing had settled into their places. Maybe I was going to lose my position, or my life, but it seemed possible that I could make some decisions from that point on. At least I had obtained some kind of free will.

"Honey," I said to Mona as she lay dejected and wretched on our couch.

"What?"

"Let's go out to dinner and then, and then let's get Seela and go to that inn you like in Montauk."

"It's Saturday," she said. "It'll be booked up."

"I'll call," I said. "If they've got a room, we could go there."

Seela answered the door wearing the same blue housecoat.

"Millie and Martin are asleep," she whispered.

"I got us a room in Montauk for tonight and tomorrow night," I said. "Come with us."

At any other time Seela would have said no. She didn't like sudden changes. But I was sure that she was in bed thinking about her transgressions, and she must have felt especially used with Martin in bed with Millie again.

Seela was a good girl and easily made to feel bad.

"Okay," she said, failing to make a smile.

"We'll be in the car out front," I told her.

I had already called Svetlana.

~

"I'm going to take Mona and Seela out to Long Island for a day," I said. "I have to get things straight with them."

"Okay," Lana said.

"That's all? Just 'okay'? Aren't you mad at me?"

"No. They are your family. I will be here—waiting."

"Lana—"

"Don't worry, Ben, darling. I am here . . . for now. You must live your own life. I will be here waiting for you."

❧

When I got down to the car, I found Mona asleep against the passenger-side window. We owned an old Citroën. It was olive green and had the look of a VW bug that had been squashed down by some heavy-footed behemoth. It had a hydraulic system that made you feel as if you were riding in a boat instead of a car. And owning a Citroën was unique; there were no other cars on the road to rival it.

I got in behind the wheel.

"Is she coming?" Mona asked.

"I thought you were asleep."

I rubbed the palms of my hands along the laced leather guard on the steering wheel. The supple and yet rough texture against my skin elated me. I was alive and still able to move forward in my own life.

"I was watching two men have sex in that doorway across the street," she said, almost wistfully. "One of them was dressed like a woman. He was fucking the other one. I was watching them and then I was in Saint Croix with my family on a vacation."

"She's getting dressed."

"What are we going to do, Ben?" Mona asked, sitting and waking up with a twist of her shoulders and torso.

132

We hadn't talked much at dinner. She was still too sad about Harvard and his sudden, inexplicable desertion.

"Why didn't you tell me about Barbara Knowland?" I said in answer to her question.

We both knew how long it took for Seela to put together her things and so it made sense to start a longer conversation. We had at least fifteen minutes' waiting time.

"Harv said that he should look into it before bothering you," she said, avoiding looking into my face.

"Had you already started your relationship then?"

Mona hesitated a long while and then whispered, "Yes."

"So you made love and then decided, or maybe it was the other way around," I speculated. "Maybe he told you to leave me flapping in the wind and then he took you up in his arms."

"You don't have to be cruel, Ben."

"Did you at least consider telling me?" I asked.

"Yes. Of course I did. But, you see, Barbara didn't call me first, she called Harv. She knew him because he had talked to her in Oakland, to see if we should do the original story on her. He's the one that told me about the accusation. Telling you would have involved him and that was just too . . . confusing."

"But, honey," I said in an evenly metered voice, "not telling me might have gotten me sent to prison for the rest of my life."

Mona looked at me sorrowfully and Seela rapped on the window. She had a bag that was filled with enough stuff to go away for a week.

"Pop the trunk, Daddy."

★　　★　　★

133

Mona and Seela slept on the long late-night drive. Or, when I think back on that night, maybe they just pretended to be asleep. Both of them had a lot on their minds. Mona betrayed me and in return was let down and deceived by both me and her lover. Seela was losing her parents, and she had in her own way betrayed those that she loved.

I worried about them on that ride, and not as distant relatives with vague problems, which is how I usually saw my wife and daughter, but as victims of my own wanton disregard.

I didn't feel guilty about what I'd said to Harvard "Harv" Rollins. A man had to do something to derail an affair like that. But all those years of quiet indifference I showed Mona and Seela had taken from them the water of life. They were dried-up seeds hoping for dew or the sweat of strangers. And I was the drought, the famine that afflicted them.

Oddly, these thoughts soothed me on that three-hour drive. I felt that my passive crimes against my parents, my wife, and daughter explained why people were after me, looking to put me in prison.

It was as if I had summoned up Barbara Knowland and Winston Meeks, Harvard Rollins and my wife's betrayal. I was guilty and this was my punishment.

Most guilty men, I'd been told many times over, see themselves as innocent; this is the tragedy of the criminal: Because of his denial of guilt, he can never learn and therefore cannot contribute to the rehabilitation, not of himself but of the world that he has wronged. But I was guilty and I knew it. Maybe I hadn't murdered Sean Messier, but I had wronged my family.

When these notions came into my mind, I laughed out loud.

The ladies roused in their slumbers, or pretenses, and then settled again.

We got a place at the beachside Montauk Manor House because someone had cancelled a reservation just an hour before I called. They left the door to our bungalow open and we tumbled in late that night, all of us going to sleep almost immediately. We didn't even take our bags from the car.

I awoke to the sound of the ocean through the open window, the susurration of waves felt as if it were calling to me.

Mona was deep asleep. She didn't stir as I climbed out of the rickety bed. I went into the common room of the suite. Seela's bag was on the broken-down blue sofa. That meant she was up and had already gone to the car.

The sliding glass doors that led to the ocean were open.

I could see my daughter walking down along the beach in shorts, her dark legs scissoring the bright sunrise.

"Hi, baby," I said, coming up to Seela.

I was barefoot, wearing gray suit pants and an old T-shirt.

"Hi, Daddy."

"What's wrong?" I asked, responding to her tone of voice.

"I don't know how to talk to you now that you found me up there with Martin."

"I already told you about me, honey, and it's not like you did something wrong, Seela. You aren't married to Jamal. Martin's not married to Millie. It was me that was wrong for even mentioning Jamal's name."

"It's not that," she said.

The cold water from the sea rolled over my bare feet and pant

135

cuffs. It crossed my mind that I would have never allowed my business clothes to get wet like that before.

"What is it then?" I asked.

"Are you going to break up with Mommy?"

"That has nothing to do with you or anything you've done."

"When Marty came over yesterday, I had no idea what was going to happen," she said. "Neither did he."

"Nothing wrong with spontaneity."

"No, but there's something wrong with me. I feel it in my shoulders and at the back of my neck," she said. "If a boy or a man touches me there, I can't help myself. When Marty put his hand on my shoulder, he was just being friendly, but after that he couldn't stop me. I've been like that ever since I was fourteen."

"With other kids at school?"

"And two teachers."

"What teachers?"

"I won't say, Daddy. They shouldn't have done it, but I'm the one who came on to them."

Again I thought about being guilty. I humiliated my daughter by shining a light on her indiscretion. Now she opened a door for me to pass through. Where was I when she was so vulnerable? Where was I when she was a child having sex with men? And why would I burden her with my troubles? I felt responsible but out of control, like when I would go out on a drinking binge in California and Colorado.

My little ugly duckling, that's what I had always thought about Seela. Could she have read my thoughts? Had I ever called her beautiful, as she was to me now? Had I looked into her eyes when she got home from having sex in the cloakroom with Mr. Hodges or maybe Mr. Rhynne?

136

My strength left me and I fell to my knees in the wet sand. Seela knelt down beside me.

"Don't tell Mommy," she said, "not ever."

"Have you written about any of this in your diary?" I asked.

"No one knows. I haven't written about it and I haven't told anyone, not a soul but you."

The cold wave on my knees sent a tremor through me. And a thought came into my mind.

"On those days that you, that you did that, what did you write in your journal?"

"I just wrote down things that happened a long time ago," she said, "or I made something up."

She was my daughter all right. She protected herself automatically, like a seasoned boxer or some amphibian hatched onshore but who instinctively knows to run for the water before the ominous shadows descend.

"Would you consider going into therapy for a while, Seel?"

"You think I'm crazy?"

"Uh-uh, no. But I do think that you feel guilty for things you've done, and if you can talk to somebody who's safe, maybe you'll learn how not to feel bad."

"But I don't feel all that bad most of the time," she said.

"Yeah, I know. But sometimes isn't it like you can't feel anything? Like there's a dead space where your life ought to be?"

The glow of realization in her eyes told me I was right. My daughter had been created out of my own cold remove.

She put her arms around my neck and I felt naked, exposed. The passion of her hug was one thing, but there was much more going on. It felt as if I were on an abandoned beach with

137

the first true love of my life. And in a way it was true. My ability to touch her was electrifying—something that I hadn't felt for so long I couldn't remember the last time it had happened. My heart was pounding. My breath was ragged and out of control.

"Daddy, you're hurting me."

"Let's go wake your mother up and get some breakfast, okay?" I said.

On our walk back to the house Seela said, "I'd like that, Daddy."

"What?"

"To see a psychologist. I'd like to talk to somebody about how I feel."

I called my own therapist after pancakes and bacon at Myrtle's Seaside Diner.

"I was waiting for you," he said.

"I'm sorry, Dr. Shriver. I needed to take my family away. They're hurting and most of it is because of me."

"What about tomorrow?"

"I don't know if we'll be back. We might stay here another day."

"If you can't make it," Shriver said, "I'll keep the appointment open. I know you're going through a lot, but try to get in to see me."

"I can't make it in the morning," I said, "but I could do it about three."

"Three then."

I hung up and Mona was standing there smiling at me. Smiling. When was the last time that had happened?

★   ★   ★

That was the last day that we were a family: Mona, Seela, and Ben. We rented a rowboat but never made it more than a hundred feet from the dock. There was a strong current that our oars couldn't master. But we laughed a lot and then spent the afternoon swimming. At least Seela and her mother did. I'm not a very good swimmer. I get frantic in the water, fearing I might sink. So I lay down on the sand and drifted in and out of wakefulness, having little naps and blinking at the sun.

❧

In one reverie I was in a garden in Colorado in the spring. I was walking with a brown and beautiful woman wearing a see-through, gossamer white dress. Her dark nipples were hard, pressing against the pale fabric. We stopped at a rosebush with large orange and red and yellow flowers. The woman leaned toward a huge rose, got the whole thing in her mouth somehow, and bit it off. As she chewed the petals, I noticed that a thorn had torn her bottom lip. She felt the pain and licked off the blood and then smiled her bloody and beautiful smile for me.

～

I awoke with a start to see my wife and daughter on their knees on either side of me.

"Take us to dinner," Mona said.

"Yeah," Seela added.

That night our daughter fell asleep early. Mona and I were still wide awake. We had gone to bed, however, because that's what we were used to doing. We had even kissed good-night but our eyes remained open.

139

I was thinking about Star Knowland and her testimony that I had murdered a man twenty-some years ago. Certainly there was the possibility in the air that I would spend the rest of my life in a Western prison. It didn't matter if I was guilty or not. I could be convicted.

Fear was gnawing at me. It was building into panic when I turned to Mona and said, "Tell me how this thing with Harvard Yard started."

"I thought this was a vacation, Ben."

"It's after midnight. By noon tomorrow you'll be back at work. He'll come to your office and you'll fall into his big, strong arms."

"It's over between us," she said, not looking at me.

"You mean, if he came to you and said he was sorry and that he loved you, you'd tell him no and spend the rest of your life with me?"

It almost was funny, how honest Mona was. She heard my words and considered them. Of course she'd run to Harvard; he was Ivy League, whereas I was just a two-year training college.

"Tell me," I said.

"Why?"

"Because I'm sitting here in the dark thinking about prison. Because you knew about Barbara Knowland and didn't even say a word. Not only that, you left me alone in the house to fend for myself when Winston Meeks was looking for me. Because you would have told him where I was if I had told you."

Mona sat up exposing her breasts. This revelation was shockingly unsexual.

"You wouldn't understand, Ben," she said.

"What?"

"I couldn't help it. I couldn't stop myself."

140

"Why wouldn't I understand that?"

"Because your whole life is like a day-planner. You wake up at the same time every day whether or not there's an alarm or clouds or sun or if the curtains are pulled. Because you go to work each day and come home every night and you're never mad or excited or frustrated. Because you never tell me that I need to do more or to be home. You never get jealous when men call and I flirt with them on the phone."

"I was jealous of Harvard Yard."

"His name is Rollins."

"I don't care what his name is."

"That was the first time," she said, "the first time you ever got the least bit jealous and I had already been fucking him for over a month."

"So tell me how it started," I said again.

Mona was seething. I was manipulating her but I didn't feel guilty about it. She could see what I was doing and I needed the friction to save me from sliding down into the hole she had helped to dig.

"Do you remember when I went to Oakland to interview Barbara Knowland for the story?" she asked.

I remembered that she'd gone out of town to do an interview but I didn't know with whom or even where. I nodded though.

"We were staying in the same hotel, Harv and I," she said. "I had some wine at dinner and he walked me up to my room. I guess I had been talking about how I wanted more life out of . . . out of you."

"Me?"

"Yes, you. And so when we got to my room, he tried to kiss me. I didn't let him, not at first. Then I said just one kiss. He hugged me

141

close then and we kissed with a lot of feeling. I pushed him away and he took my purse and found my key card. He opened the door and kind of shoved me into the room. I couldn't help it, Ben. It made me gasp. Wherever I turned, he was there. And I was feeling him. Do you hate me?"

I pulled aside the blankets to show her my erection. Without another word she climbed up on it. The shock of entering her was something I hadn't felt since I was a teenager. She looked into my eyes, grinning while she bounced her hard buttocks against my thighs. Every time I came close to orgasm, she stopped and stared at me as if I were a stranger to her.

"Do you know why I was so upset the night you fucked my ass?" she whispered.

I shook my head, astonished by the language she was using, the language she learned from other lovers.

"Do you know why I was bleeding?"

"No," I gasped.

"Because I had just let Harv do that to me that morning in my office. I made him wear a condom but I was still so scared. He held his hand over my mouth and whispered things to me."

"What?" I asked. I didn't want to but I couldn't help myself.

"He'd tell me when he was going to press deeper," she said, "when he was going to give me more of his cock."

The hunger and pleasure in her voice were completely alien to me. It was as if I were with some other woman.

"Come," she said, seeing the orgasm build in me. She grabbed my hair and sneered at me. "Give it to me," she whispered, and I screamed and lurched under her like some machine that had slipped its gears and was coming apart under its own force.

★   ★   ★

142

We were strangers again in the morning. On the long ride back Seela talked to Mona about her classes and her friends in school. The things she said were probably true but I knew that they were a shield for my daughter's real feelings and experiences.

I dropped Mona at our apartment and then took Seela down to her place.

"Are you going to be all right, Daddy?" Seela asked before getting out.

"Are you all right?" I asked back.

"I'll be okay. But what about you and Mommy?"

"We'll be okay, honey. We'll make it. Maybe we won't be together, but we'll make it."

By the time I had parked in the lot and walked back to our place, Mona was gone.

There was a light blinking on the answering machine. There were eight messages, all from Harvard Rollins.

"Mona," he said in the first one, "I'm sorry. Let's talk."

The installments got more and more intense until he said that he was going to call his friends at the police department to make sure that she was okay.

That's what dragged Mona out of the house. His passion and need, his love and willingness to act.

I felt bereft. Maybe, I thought, Mona had made such deep love to me so that we could both know what we were giving up. It wasn't Rollins but our last bout of lovemaking that sounded the death knell of our relationship. As long as we didn't say anything, didn't get close enough to see who we really were, there was a chance that we could remain together. But now it was done. It was not possible for me to give her what Harvard Rollins could provide. And now that I knew

143

about him, I could see too clearly into the fantasies my wife had to keep her from going mad.

At noon I picked up the phone and dialed.

"Hello?"

"Hi, Mom."

"Ben," she said, and then she paused for maybe half a minute. In those thirty seconds she swallowed the years of anger and complaints. I could almost hear the unspoken grievances smothered in the silence on the line.

"How are you, Ben?" she asked at last.

"Okay, Mom. What about you?"

"I'm all right," she said in a voice too high.

"I'm sorry about the other day," I said. "I got a lot on my mind and when you kept on ragging on me, I just couldn't take it."

"What's wrong?"

"Why did Dad used to hit me and Briggs so much, Mama?"

"Is that it? Is that what's bothering you? Your father's discipline?"

"Discipline? He whipped us with that strap until we were covered with welts, and we never did anything wrong."

"Never did?" she said. "You were defiant. You disobeyed. You, you ran in the streets."

"We were always home by four."

"You were supposed to be there by three thirty. Don't you understand? He had to stay on you like that. If he hadn't, you might have turned out bad."

"Like Briggs?" I asked.

That started my mother crying. It had been many years. I'd forgotten the tears, her defense against male anger.

"Did beating Briggs keep him from dealing drugs?" I asked.

"Why are you persecuting me?" my mother asked. "Why are you saying these things? We only tried to raise you right."

"By Dad beating one of us every other week? By him threatening us with beatings every day? By him refusing to let Briggs stay at home after they arrested him that first time?"

"Your father had to teach Briggs a lesson," my mother said. "He couldn't spank him anymore. He was a man. And, and we had to worry about you."

"By taking away my brother?" I said

"You don't understand."

"All right," I said. "Maybe I don't get it. Maybe he was trying to do something that I missed, that Briggs missed."

My mother was the depth of night on the other end of the line—silence and darkness made up the whole of her presence.

"So let me ask you a question to see if maybe we can talk about this a little . . . Mom?"

"Yes," she uttered.

"Let's say Pop didn't like pork chops," I said. "Let's say he hated pork chops. He told you never to put pork chops on the table when he came home to eat."

"But your father loved pork," my mother said from a field of fond memory.

"But let's say he didn't."

"Okay. But he did, you know."

"And so one day," I continued, "you found this recipe for pork chops that you were sure he was going to love. You spend the whole day making these very special pork chops. And when he gets home and he sees those chops on the table, he grabs you by the hair . . ."

"No."

". . . he grabs you by the hair and throws you on the bed. He takes off all your clothes until you're buck naked and he twists your arm so that if you try to squirm it hurts like hell . . ."

"No!"

". . . and then he pulls off his strap with one hand and whips you and whips you until there's welts all up and down your legs and your body . . ."

"No."

". . . and when you say, 'Please stop,' he tells you that he asked you not to make pork chops but did that stop you? And he keeps on beating you until your arm feels like it's breaking and your body feels like it's on fire."

"Please, Ben, stop."

I heard my own plea in her voice. I was my father using my tongue as the strap. The receiver in my hand was her arm all twisted and mangled.

"Would that be okay, Mom? If he did that to you like he did to Briggs and me. Would you have stood quiet and forgiven him?"

I expected her to hang up on me this time. The susurrous sounds made by some soft friction on her end made me think that she was quivering with rage and sorrow. I had said everything I had ever wanted to. I was ready to give up on my mother.

"You never understood your father, Ben. He had a hard life, a scary life. Nobody ever showed him the slightest bit of love after he was seven and his parents and sisters died in the fire. He loved you and Briggs more than anything, and all he ever wanted was to make you boys into men."

What she said was no doubt true. Rage stoked the fires of his love, but it was still love. He worked twelve-hour days and never

146

bowed down under the weight of his responsibilities. He never abandoned his family. The beatings were filled with his passion for us. I could see that.

"I have to go now, Mom," I said.

"You must forgive him, Ben."

"Would you forgive him if he beat you like that?"

"I would have rather he did it to me than you, Ben. I would have taken your punishment if I could, because seeing your pain was the worst thing in my life. I stood by because the only other thing I could have done was to take you away. And if I did that, your father would have died."

It was the truth. I knew it. My father, who loved me as much as nuns love God, had to beat me in order to stave off the demons that bedeviled him. And my mother had to watch or to kill him. The only other answer would be that I was never born, that some other child had taken my place in my father's torture chamber of love.

There on the east side of Midtown I sat with the phone pressed to my ear. Thousands of miles away my mother sat in the same pose. Both of us were silent, both of us grieved for the love we did know.

Time passed effortlessly in the face of that shared, silent misery. I realized that I had no notion of what my mother felt. I understood that I could have gone to my father's funeral. I could have gotten on a plane and said good-bye.

I had never been to his grave site, never sent flowers or even asked what was written on his stone. Maybe my name was there . . . *Derek Dibbuk survived by Briggs and Ben*. I didn't even know if my father had a middle name.

They say we live in the most advanced culture in the history of the world. But there I was, more ignorant than any lump of coal.

147

"Ben?" my mother said.

"Yeah, Mom?"

"You have to let it go, baby."

"But, Mom," I said. "It's all I have. I've hated Dad every day since I can remember. I never think about it. But all he ever was to me was a beating waiting to happen. He broke Briggs. That's why I used to call you, to try to explain why I drank and ran around so much."

"But you cleaned up," my mother said. "You got a good job and gave us a grandchild. Your father was very happy about that."

"I didn't clean up, Mom. I gave up. I stopped feeling. At least when I was drunk I was feeling something."

"I feel sorry for you then, baby," she said.

I hung up.

On Dr. Shriver's couch I continued thinking about my dead father.

". . . he would tell us stories about when he was a tough down in Texas," I was saying, "but when we asked him how life was when he was a child like us, he got all broody and quiet. If we pushed too much, one of us would have ended up getting a whipping."

"Did you love your father?" Adrian Shriver asked.

"Not in the way I wanted to."

"What does that mean?"

"I loved him because I needed him . . . for my survival," I said. "I needed him to save me and at the same time not to beat me. I needed him for food and shelter and protection against the outside world. But I never loved him for who he was. He scared me. He came from a world that I never wanted to see. He was angry and drunk and smelled like cigarettes."

"You smell like tobacco now," Dr. Shriver said.

"These cigarettes are more important than therapy," I said. "If I didn't have them, I'd go mad."

"How would that look?"

"I'd get violent. I'd, I'd holler and shout. I'd go out and kill Harvard Rollins for sleeping with my wife. I'd kill her too . . . just for good measure."

"Would you really?" he asked.

I sat up on the sofa, clasping my hands tightly. I looked at the gentle doctor. My reflection in the lenses of his glasses hid his eyes from me. I stared at myself, my hands grasping at each other.

"That is the central question of my entire life, Adrian," I said, his first name unfamiliar on my tongue. "Would I actually lose control? Could I? Have I?"

The therapist shifted his head and his eyes came into view. There was sympathy in that gaze, real concern.

"And the answer is," I said in my imitation of a game show host, "I don't have the slightest idea."

"And so when Barbara Knowland suggested that you committed some heinous crime, you believed that it might be true."

"It echoed with something deep inside of me," I said. "My mother said to me just today that my father beat me because he loved me. What kind of lesson is that?"

"Your mother is still alive?"

"Yeah. Didn't I ever tell you that?"

"No."

"Did I tell you that my father died seven years ago and that I didn't go to his funeral because I had too much work?"

★   ★   ★

"Mr. Dibbuk," a serious and masculine voice announced.

"Yes?"

I was coming out the front door of the therapy office. This door was a few feet below the sidewalk. The men were waiting for me at the top of the stairs.

"Officer Bandell," the white man who called to me said, identifying himself. He was showing me a badge and an ID card in an open wallet. "I'm sorry but you'll have to come with us."

Mona had heard me on the phone. That was the only way they could have known I'd be there that afternoon.

There were two cops with Bandell: one black, the other Asian. The Asian man put handcuffs on me. The black officer took me by the arm. I was in the custody of the military arm of the Rainbow Coalition. Soon I'd be thrown at the feet of Jesse Jackson and asked to repent my antisocial ways.

They locked me in a cell with a middle-aged man like myself, only he was white and short, silent as a stump, and almost without affect. He sat on the corner of his cot, across from me, staring off into space—less like a thinker and more like a coma victim or maybe even an open-eyed corpse.

The officers said very little to me on the way to the precinct. They told me before taking my belongings that I was being held for up to seventy-two hours while someone higher up was considering my case.

"What case?" I asked them.

"I have no idea," Officer Bandell replied.

They took my fingerprints and my shoelaces. They itemized the contents of my pockets and took down my name, social security number, date of birth, and home address.

There were no bars on our cell. The door was metal, painted green, and solid. There was only a slit that I could look out through. If my roommate wanted to kill me or I wanted him dead, there was no one to stop us.

I didn't find out the squat white man's name. He never even spoke a proper sentence to me.

"How you doin'?" I said to him upon entering the cell.

"Huh," he replied with a nod.

"Dibbuk?" a man said.

I woke up out of a completely dreamless sleep. My summoner wore a gray uniform with a hat that you'd expect to see on someone who worked for the railroad.

"That's me," I said, trying to get my head straight.

"Come on."

He turned and left the cell. I followed. Three other men were waiting for me outside. One wore a blue uniform; the other three were clad in gray. They surrounded me in diamond formation, their protection unbreakable. They didn't even bind my hands.

We went down an extraordinarily long hall of green cell doors and lighter green walls, turned a corner, and walked down a hall the same length again. Then we came to a huge elevator. The man who retrieved me from the cell pressed one of the middle buttons. The elevator moved so slowly I didn't know if we were going up or down.

We came out into a large square room that was lined by doors on all sides. They brought me to an office in the far-right corner. One of my guards opened the door and I entered, wondering if I could have subdued those men and made my escape if I were some great martial arts master.

Sitting behind a very messy desk was a huge-faced white man with a pink wart on his nose. His nameplate said BILL TORNAY. Tornay was reading a file, maybe mine, and scowling hideously.

"Sit," he said without looking at me.

There was one chair but it had a few dozen manila folders on it. I wondered if I should remove the folders or just sit on them.

The monster looked up at me after a few beats of indecision.

"I said, sit down."

I sat on the folders.

"Ben Arna Dibbuk," he said. "Is 'Ben' short for 'Benjamin'?"

"No, it's not."

"What are you in here for, Dibbuk?"

There was an odd scent in the air. I didn't know if it was the man or just his environment, but it was a sour odor that had a ripe edge to it. I felt my butt slipping on the slick folders.

"I have no idea," I said, scooting backward in the chair. "Officer Bandell just picked me up and said that they were going to hold me."

"Did he allow you a phone call?"

"No."

"Did he read you your rights?"

"He never asked me anything and he said almost as little."

My turn of phrase caught the ugly man's attention.

"It says here that you're a computer programmer," he said. "Where do you work?"

"Our Bank."

"Are you in trouble there?"

"Not that I know of."

He studied my face, looking for signs of criminality or depravity. He leaned back and the office chair cried out as if in pain.

"Do you want to make a call?" he asked.

"Do you know what time it is?" I had lost track of the hour.

"Eleven fifteen."

"Tuesday morning?"

That got the man to smile. He was even uglier when showing good humor.

He called to the men in the hall and they took me to a corridor of pay phones. One of them handed me a quarter and they let me loose among the dozen or more little cubbies that contained the phones. The corridor was actually a cul-de-sac, so they didn't have to worry about me running away.

"Hello?"

"Hey, brother man," I said.

"Ben," Cassius Copeland said with real happiness in his tone. "Where are you?"

I told him about my arrest. He took down all the information I could give him and said that he'd look for a lawyer. After he hung up, I sat there for a while longer, pretending to speak to someone in low tones. I didn't want to go back to that cell. As long as I was in there, it was okay, but now that I was out, I wanted to stay out.

Finally I knew I had to get off. I hung up and went back to the jail guards.

In my cell again I wondered about Mona. She was definitely with Harvard again. Sex with him would always be better. She was even fucking him while using me for the cock. But maybe she hadn't actually betrayed me. Maybe she had mentioned about the therapist and he passed the information on without her knowledge.

I didn't hate her for loving someone else; I was just lonely. My daughter most likely didn't even know that I was missing. I felt completely alone in that cell. I think I would have cried if my silent cellmate weren't there.

I wondered if this was how it would be in Colorado once I was convicted for the murder I may or may not have committed. Would I just be sitting on a cot staring into space, counting the days, looking forward to rice pudding on Friday nights and letters from my daughter?

She would get married, have kids, and send me photographs. I would look at those pictures, feeling distant, disconnected. But I'd write letters telling her how beautiful the children were and I'd send them little gifts that I'd make in the wood shop or metal shop that the prison afforded.

I spent the rest of my jail time having fantasies like that. I thought about my mother coming and apologizing for her negligence. I thought about my brother getting out of prison and him coming to visit me so that he could gloat over how far I'd fallen.

"You were always the one they liked more," he'd tell me.

"They never liked either one of us," I'd say to Briggs. "We were both failed experiments—like Frankenstein's monster or American democracy."

A few hours after I'd been to see him, the green metal door opened and Bill Tornay entered. The cell stank from my roommate's use of the commode. I was embarrassed that the warden coming in would think I had made that smell.

I had closed my eyes while my cellmate took his grunting shit. We'd had two meals; powdered eggs for breakfast and bologna sandwiches on white bread for lunch.

"Mr. Dibbuk," the hippopotamus-faced ugly man said, "come with me."

He was alone. Standing up he was more of an oddity than he was behind the scrim of refuse piled on his desk. He had small, slender shoulders while his legs were huge, shapeless pillars of flesh. He walked as an elephant might if an elephant stood upright on two legs. It was a shambling, side-to-side motion that had very little to do with everyday humanity.

The sour-ripe smell did come from Tornay. It wafted behind him, making me want to take the lead. But I couldn't do that. I was a prisoner; I would be for the rest of my life.

We took the long halls again, rode in the elevator again, but this time we exited into a room that had sunlight in it. We went to an office, where a white man in a sharp dark suit stood.

"Mr. Dibbuk," the man said.

"Yes."

"I'm Agent Lawry. I'm with the FBI."

"What does the FBI want with me?" I asked.

Bill Tornay was already gone. The door closed behind him.

"The FBI has no interest in you, sir," Lawry said. "I'm just here to take you somewhere."

"Where?"

"You'll see."

After giving me my things back, Agent Lawry took me to the police garage. He drove a black Ford. There were no frills in the company car. It seemed like a rental; impersonal and clean.

Lawry was of medium height and in shape. He had no facial hair, pimples, or blemishes. His brown hair was cut short, but not too short. Once we were in the car, his sentences were all five words or less.

For all his studied anonymity, the FBI man had a very peculiar

155

face. It was both flat and thin. This seemed like a contradiction. Long faces needed to come out and flat ones belonged on round heads. If I had ever seen Lawry on a street or across a room, I would have remembered his odd mug.

I asked him questions about my arrest and him coming to retrieve me. His answers were all short and meaningless.

He'd driven us for a dozen minutes, no more, when we came to a stop. I was surprised to see that we were parked in front of Joey Bondhauser's Steak House.

"Here you go," Lawry said.

"So we're finished?"

His only reply was a nod.

"Ben!" fat Joey said in greeting.

He was sitting at the bar, drinking from a large glass of clear liquid.

My hand disappeared into his powerful, fleshy grip.

He pulled me to a bar stool, where I perched nervously.

The ex–intelligence officer had brown eyes and brown hair that was probably dyed. His face was very round, rotund actually. His smile held no warmth or even mirth, but that seemed to me an honest expression. He didn't know me; why feel all personal and cuddly?

"Cass says you got problems," Joey said.

"Yeah."

"Between him and me, we've seen a whole world of trouble," Bondhauser confided. "Magda."

"Yes, Mr. Bondhauser."

Magda was wearing a red dress that day. She was so beautiful that I could imagine someone aching just by looking at her.

156

"Make the rooms ready for Mr. Dibbuk here. He'll be meeting Cassius Copeland up there."

"Yes, sir."

When she turned away, I felt a little sad. My time in jail, however long it was, had made me feel that I would never behold beauty again. There was a feeling growing in my chest. It was like a small sphere of radiant energy, pulsing out of sequence with my heartbeat. After a moment I realized that this feeling was yearning—something that I had never allowed myself to feel as an adult.

"You want a drink, Ben?"

"Yes, I do."

"What's your poison?"

I wanted to say cognac, cognac in a big snifter with a lime peel on a dish at the side. And not just one snifter, but many of them over the next few days, while the police searched for me and while my wife rutted with the detective—rich amber liquor moving through my veins like chamber music on a sunny afternoon in a many-windowed room in July.

"Cranberry juice," I said. "No ice but a twist of lime."

Bondhauser called the order over to his bartender. There was a hint of disappointment in his tone.

"Cass is a great friend of mine," Joey said then.

"He's a good guy."

Joey looked at me, pondering my diffident reply.

"Lotta good guys in the world, Ben," he said. "Work friends, drinking buddies, guys who'll lie to your wife when you need 'em to. But a great friend, a friend like Cass, is there when you need him and he's there for the long haul.

"There was a time once when I was out on my own. My boys

157

didn't want me and their enemies wanted me dead"—it seemed as if Joey was staring straight through my forehead, into my mind—"I was what they call persona non grata. And Cass was the only man in the world who would go to bat for me.

"I'm not talkin' about raisin' his voice and complaining. He put his ass on the line. And when it was all over, and I was back in the saddle, he didn't even ask for a—for an extra nickel or the slightest consideration.

"You see how he eats at the counter here?"

I nodded as the bartender brought my red drink.

"He doesn't have to do that. I let all my old friends, the ones that abandoned me, eat at the bar. But Cass knows that he could come up to my house any day and eat up in the bed with my wife and kids. He could have my whole damn house, my bank account, and I wouldn't flinch. Cass is a great friend. There's not enough gold in the Federal Reserve to pay for something like that."

I said nothing to all this. Bondhauser had gotten passionate over his notions of Cass, and even though I agreed with him, I didn't believe anything I could say would match his fervor.

"And so," Joey said, "when Cass comes to me and tells me that one of his best friends is in trouble, I stand up. I call the FBI. I tell my man there, Heydrich Lawry, that I need him to come up with some pretext to bring that man out of the tombs.

"Don't get me wrong, Ben. *You* don't owe me a damn thing. I did all of that because of Cass. He's the real article and I owe him big."

Magda came up behind her voluminous employer. I was glad to see her. Joey Bondhauser's emotional demonstration made me nervous. I didn't know what to say or even how to sit or hold my hands.

"The rooms are ready, sir," she said.

"Good," Joey said to her while looking at me.

He gripped my hand again and brought his face close to mine.

"I will go as far as Cass asks me to help you, Ben. Don't forget that."

The "rooms" made up a beautiful suite on the top floor of the skyscraper that housed Joey Bondhauser's Steak House. The sitting room had a western view. The Hudson was prominent and buildings leading uptown glittered in the afternoon sun.

"Would you like me to stay with you?" pale-eyed Magda asked.

"Don't you have to be at work?"

"Mr. Bondhauser says that you are my most important job today." Her look was both defiant and submissive.

"Wow. Imagine that. A lowly computer programmer tended by a woman worth ten of him."

"What can I do for you?" she said in the same mild accent that Svetlana had.

"I'll call the restaurant if I want anything," I said. "Right now all I need to do is rest."

Magda nodded and left the room.

I went to the window and stared at the stone and steel, the glass and smatterings of flesh that made up my adopted city. My fingers were tingling, and if I closed my eyes, I was back in that cell with the man who never spoke. The smell of the jailer who had released me was still in my nostrils.

I thought about Cass's offer to kill Star Knowland. Her death would have probably vouchsafed my freedom. That, along with the view, brought to mind the scene in the movie *The Third Man* where Orson Welles asks Joseph Cotten, what difference would it make if one of the tiny ants so far below stopped moving?

159

Very little, I thought, but still I couldn't be the one to give the order. I could not ask for her death. I didn't believe that I had murdered a man. If I had, wouldn't I be able to kill Star, a real enemy?

"Hello?" she said.

"Hey, Lana. How are you?"

"Ben. Where have you been? I thought you'd be back yesterday."

I told her about my arrest.

"Are they going to take you to Colorado?" she asked me.

"I don't know. But will you meet me at the hotel tonight?"

"Yes. I have missed you. I want to make love."

There were many books on the shelves of Joey Bondhauser's little getaway. He had the complete works of Dickens, Twain, Hugo, Balzac, Conrad, Zola, James, and many others. One shelf was stacked with modern, well-read paperbacks. I got the feeling that Joey let many people stay in his "rooms." The classics on his shelves were probably put there by some designer, but the paperbacks were brought in by his guests.

I glanced through these soft-cover books, uncharacteristically drawn to the stories told. I read the first few pages of a couple of thrillers, but they didn't grab me. There was one book, however, among the mysteries and nonfiction hits, that struck a note. It was a book called *The Night Man*, about a guy, a kind of mortal vampire, who only went out after the sun set. His name was Juvenal Nyx and he abhorred the daylight because of a philosophical turn of mind. It was a story, of course, about unrequited love. Juvenal fell for a woman who was a painter, a

160

watercolorist, a child of light. The fiber of him was antithetical to everything she thought and believed, but he loved her anyway.

It was a silly story, really, contrived to an absurd degree. Even the names announced themselves as symbols and metaphors. But for some reason I found myself identifying with the man that lived in darkness.

The doorbell was a small line from some piano sonata. When I first heard it, I thought that a radio alarm had gone off. But when the musical phrase repeated, I went to the door.

Cass was standing there. Unexpectedly for both of us, I put my arms around him and held on tight.

"That's okay, brother," he said as I released him, looking sheepish. "Jail's a bitch, 'specially when you ain't been there before."

We went to the living room and sat. The way Cass was dressed was unusual for him. Instead of black on black he wore a dark blue business suit with a yellow shirt, a burgundy tie, and ruby cufflinks. He smelled of sweet cologne and carried a fancy red-brown leather briefcase. After asking me about "my head," he got up and concocted a drink from gin, orange juice, seltzer, cranberry juice, and a powder that I didn't recognize. He made this drink at the stand-up bar placed at the end of the bookcase.

"You got trouble, Ben," Cass said after he was seated again.

"No kidding."

The security chief reached into his briefcase and came out with an edition of *Diablerie*. It must have been the second issue, because the first, I knew, had a picture of Lena Hess, the new singing sensation from France, on its cover.

This copy sported a glamour-mug portrait of Michael Lord

161

Hampton. He was a rapper before but now was making a name for himself as a serious actor. He was a handsome man—dark and deadly-looking.

Superimposed in red upon his blue jumpsuit was the headline, DIABLERIE EDITOR'S HUSBAND SUSPECT IN 20-YEAR-OLD COLORADO MURDER CASE.

The brief article was on page 36:

It was learned last week that Ben Arna Dibbuk, husband of *Diablerie*'s own Mona Valeria, is being investigated for the murder of Sean Messier 24 years ago in a Denver suburb. Dibbuk, a computer programmer for Our Bank, was implicated by Barbara Knowland, who was featured only last week in these pages. Knowland claims that she was present when Dibbuk murdered Messier and that he had come to two of her readings and to her hotel room trying to extort money from her by saying that he would implicate her in the crime.

Denver D.A. Winston Meeks is in New York investigating these allegations.

Another man, Grant Timmons, had been convicted of the crime and spent more than 20 years in prison. He died in state custody two years ago.

There was no byline but I was sure that Mona had written it. And she would have had to have done it before we went away to Montauk. Seeing her words damning me in a national publication almost defeated me. I was going down and my wife was helping secure the weights to my ankles.

"That's a bitch," Cass said when I looked up.

162

"In more ways than one."

"How could she do that to you?"

"I don't really understand," I said. "It's almost as if she hated me. But I haven't done anything to warrant that much, um, passion from her."

"What do you want to do, Ben?"

"If I go to my therapist, will they arrest me again?"

"Probably."

"I have an appointment with him at six today. Do you think Joey has a phone that can't be traced here?"

"We could come up with something," Cass said. "But what can a therapist do? You got to spill some blood, man."

"No. I don't know what happened yet."

"It doesn't matter what happened," Cass argued. "Some bitch wants to put you in prison, for a long time. And you know they're gonna try to blame you for this guy that died in jail. You need to act."

"Just get me a phone, Cass. I'll tell you what I want to do by tomorrow."

Cass left and a while later Magda brought me a beat-up old cell phone.

"Mr. Bondhauser says that this is what you wanted," she said.

"Yes," Shriver said, answering his office phone.

"I can't make it in today, Doc," I said. "I hoped we could do this on the phone."

"Why can't you come in?"

"The police want to arrest me."

"For what?"

"I think it's that Colorado wants to extradite me and the NYPD

163

has offered to hold on to me for a while. There weren't any charges."

"It's hard to do deep therapy over the phone, Mr. Dibbuk."

"What if I lie down and close my eyes while we talk?" I asked.

"We can try."

"I'm worried that maybe I killed somebody, Adrian," I said. "This Barbara Knowland says I did."

"Do you believe her?"

"I don't know. I mean, at first I didn't even think I knew her. I still don't remember. But then she seemed to know me and I wondered why would she lie about all this?"

"That's a good question. Why would someone lie about you?"

"Do you think I could kill somebody, Doctor?"

"Yes," he said without hesitation. "There's a rage against your father in you. With that level of anger, anything is possible."

"Why can't I remember?"

"There could be many reasons," Shriver said. "You may simply have blacked out because of the drinking. You said that there might have been a struggle, maybe you were struck in the head and experienced limited amnesia. And of course none of it may have ever happened. Barbara Knowland might have her own reasons for blaming you."

"How can I get my memories back?" I asked.

"Are you sure you want to remember?"

"Yes. More than anything."

"Okay," Shriver said. "Every morning when you wake up, sit in a comfortable chair with your eyes closed and think about Barbara Knowland's face. Can you get a picture of her when she was younger?"

"Yes. There's one in her book."

"Every morning concentrate on that face for a minute and then close your eyes. Try to summon her up in your memory."

"We could leave the country," Svetlana said at three in the morning.

We had not made love. My mind was elsewhere.

"Where could we go?"

"Europe. I speak many languages. Asia. I have always wanted to live in Brazil during Carnival."

"What about international relations?" I asked.

She shrugged and brought two cigarettes to her mouth. She lit both and put one between my lips.

"Things are always changing," she said. "I wanted to come to America so that life would be like Disney World. You know . . . everything safe and nice. But then I meet you and I am forced to love you. Love is not something you can say no to. You can quit a job or a club or even a country, but you cannot quit love."

I looked at her thin legs, her dense and golden public hair. I tried then to summon up in my mind some resentment about Sergei. Hadn't Lana betrayed me too? Yes. But I couldn't be angry with her. I couldn't afford the pain.

But neither could I call up the love that she was talking about.

"You can learn to love me," Svetlana said.

"Can you read my mind too?" I asked.

"Only your face," she said smiling. "You look so worried when you can't love me back."

"I don't understand."

"What do you want from me?" Svetlana asked.

"Nothing."

165

"No. This cannot be. Love is jealous and what do you call it . . . small-minded. You must want something from me. My body, my money, my freedom."

"But what if I wanted you to feel pain?" I asked, not knowing where the question came from.

"Then I suffer for you."

"But that's not good."

"Love is not good," she said with intense disgust on her face and in her voice. "It is not a little boy turning in his homework. Love is when you fuck me in the ass and my blood and my shit is on your cock and on my sheets and I clean you and my bedclothes and I am happy doing this. I am happy to have you back even when you have been with another woman. I am happy when you ask me to leave my husband and my children to go running where men are trying to kill us."

Lana was breathing hard. She took a deep draw on her cigarette.

"Love is when I call you in the bed with your wife and tell you to come to me."

She was lying. No, not lying, but saying what she thought I needed to hear. And she was right. I needed an example of someone giving up everything for another.

"And if I go to prison in Colorado?" I asked.

"You must ask me to come with you to see if I love you."

"But you'd be throwing away your life."

"No . . . I wouldn't," she said.

This answer was enigmatic but I had no desire to decipher it.

I leaned over and kissed her between her breasts. She crushed out her cigarette, then mine, and hugged me like a man hugs a woman.

★   ★   ★

In the morning I thought about young Star Knowland. I imagined her, tried to remember her for over an hour. I got nowhere and so I took out the beat-up cell phone that Magda gave me and called information.

"Plaza Hotel. How may I direct your call?" a woman asked.

"Winston Meeks," I said.

"One moment please."

"Hello."

"Ben Dibbuk here, Mr. Meeks."

The straight line of words stopped there for a moment. Meeks was shocked into silence.

"Where are you?" he asked slowly, deliberately.

"I'm willing to be debriefed here in New York," I said.

"My boss now says that he would like to see you in Denver."

"One step at a time, Mr. D.A. Promise me that I can leave and that you will not get the police to arrest me and I'll come over, today if you like."

"How can I get in touch with you?"

"You can't."

"Call me back in two hours," he said. "Call me then and I'll tell you."

Lana went off to school and I sat in the bed thinking about love. I was almost happy that I'd run into Star Knowland. She opened my life up like an overripe fig. I had been festering inside. I was rotting and didn't even know it.

I believed that I could never really love anyone but now I saw that I could if I allowed myself to feel the pain. This was a wholly new concept for me and it was astonishing that a virtual child had shown me the way. My careless generosity with her, my callous

167

treatment of her life, created something that marital vows and fatherhood had not given me.

It was almost beyond belief that I could have lived for forty-seven years in backward stupidity about something as simple as this.

My father beat me and I loved him for it. Not in spite of the pain but because he touched me with care, no matter how violently. He needed me to crawl and so I crawled. He needed me to hide from the light of others' feelings and so I built myself a shell out of alcohol and then later with that feeling in my shoulders.

It didn't matter. I had loved him from the first moment we met. I would keep on loving him until breath left me.

I called Cass at Our Bank and asked him to ask Joey for one more favor.

"Sure thing, buddy," he said. "It's no fun around here without you."

"We are willing to make the deal," Winston Meeks told me.

"Okay," I said. "A lawyer will call you this afternoon at four. He will lay down the terms for any meeting I agree to take. When he calls me and tells me that it's okay, I'll come over."

"You don't need a lawyer just to talk to us, Mr. Dibbuk."

"Oh yes I do. And you know it too."

It took three days to work out the agreement. Meeks had to promise to leave the NYPD out of it and also to allow a "crew" (Cass's word, not mine) to come with me to the Plaza suite.

In that time I got my life together as much as I could.

I went to Augie's coffee shop at four fifteen on Friday afternoon. Mona was there. Her visits to that coffee shop were like my tight regimen of going to work. If I had wanted to kill her, I could have

168

done it then. I thought about it but there was no reason really. Svetlana had taught me something about love—enough to know that I had never really experienced it as an adult. I couldn't blame Mona for that. I asked her if she knew about the article they published on me.

"Yes," she said, once again holding her phantom cigarette.

"Did you write it?"

She seemed like a computer program in a loop then. Her face and hands were stock-still; her eyes didn't even blink.

"Yes," she said, looking down. "What of it?"

"Are you back with Harvard Yard?"

"His name is Rollins."

"I know what the fuck his name is. I even know that you lick the end of his cock and tell him how much you like the taste."

Mona made to rise but I took hold of her forearm.

"Let me go."

"This is the last time we're ever going to speak, Mona. Let me get a little angry, huh?"

"What are you talking about?"

"I'm going to see the D.A. from Denver tomorrow. He'll try to figure out if I should be extradited and put on trial. So either I'll be in jail or otherwise gone."

"What about Seela?"

"Why didn't you tell Seela's father that there was a woman who was blaming him for a murder that he doesn't know anything about?"

Mona's face shifted then. It dawned on me that she had had a strange look on her face ever since she'd heard Star's story.

"You think I did it?" I said.

"You didn't?"

169

"I have no idea. I didn't remember her. I certainly don't remember killing anyone."

An unspoken, maybe even unconscious, apology crossed her face. She brought her fingers to her lips, the invisible cigarette forgotten.

"How could we be together for so many years and have this little trust?" I asked her.

"Harv said that there had to be something to it. Barbara knew too much about you."

It's funny how words are so delicate and still powerful. I could see Star at that moment lying across a couch or a bed. She was naked, big boned but young and also handsome. I did know her back then.

"But that doesn't mean I killed anybody."

"But . . ." Mona said. Here we were having our last verbal joust and she had just lost.

I smiled, relishing the empty victory.

"Could it be that you betrayed me because you love him, Mona?" I asked. "That all those years we spent building this life were nothing?"

"You never loved me, Benny," she said.

"No. But we made Seela, we made a home for her."

"I was sure that you were a murderer," she said. "I was frightened."

"Because if you told me, you thought I might have to kill you?" I asked. "Because you never knew me and you were afraid of your own mistakes?"

"I just didn't feel safe," she said. "That's all."

I was intent on allowing Mona to have the last word. It seemed right, especially since I had won our last argument.

I stood up from the stool. She touched my forearm.

"Where are you going?"

"That's not really up to me, honey."

"You smell like cigarettes," she said, and I turned away.

We'd probably see each other again. In lawyers' offices, in courts, at our daughter's graduation if I was free, but the relationship ended there. I could feel it.

Svetlana made a home for me in her apartment. She cooked every night and bought me new clothes. When I tried to tell her that I might go away to prison, she wouldn't listen.

"You and I are in love," she'd say. "God wouldn't take something like that away."

"Do you believe in God?" I asked.

"He believes in me," she said with unqualified conviction.

We set the meeting with Winston Meeks for that Saturday. I overslept but that was my only symptom of fear. I met Cass's "crew" at a coffee shop around the corner. Cass was wearing black slacks and a black turtleneck, like I was used to seeing him in.

The security expert was accompanied by Leonard Gideon, a bald white man with enough hair on his lip to make up for what was missing up top. He was bursting with energy that teetered on the verge of rage. Gideon was my lawyer. He shook my hand and asked a few questions, then he smiled under that bale of mustache, saying, "We're gonna kick their asses, Arna, all the way from here back to the Rocky Mountains."

Accompanying Cass and the lawyer was Charles Milford. Milford worked for the federal government in some capacity that was not clear to me. But Cass assured me that no city or state entity could arrest me if Milford objected.

★   ★   ★

171

Meeks's suite was on the ninth floor. It should have been called an apartment it was so big. There were seven people waiting for us: the stenographer, two Colorado marshals, two female assistants from Meeks's office, and the lie detector expert. The machine itself was set up on a table next to a plain pine chair. For some reason the setup brought to mind the electric chair. That made real the worry that I could be executed for the crime Star Knowland said I committed.

Gideon started the conversation. He presented Meeks with a stack of papers to sign. Whenever the Western D.A. balked, Gideon threatened to leave with his client, me.

After the preliminaries were done, Meeks and I sat across from each other surrounded by our seconds.

"Did you kill Sean Messier?"

"No," I said, thinking, *not to my knowledge.*

"Did you know him?"

"No." Again with the sentence finished in my mind.

"Did you hit him with a heavy metal object?"

"I just told you that I didn't know him," I said. "How could I have hit him if I didn't know him?"

I could make out Gideon's smile through the thatch of his mustache.

"Do you mind taking a lie detector test?"

"No. But I want to know something first."

"What's that?"

"That machine scares me. This whole thing is very anxiety provoking. How can you tell the difference between me being scared and me lying?"

The lie detector expert, who had been introduced to me as Roger, spoke up then. He was a short guy with bright eyes and facial hair that failed to become either a proper beard or mustache.

"We screen your emotions with test questions distributed throughout the interrogation," Roger told me. "In other words, we factor in your fear quotient."

"How accurate is it?"

"If you're a sociopath or a deranged psychotic, it won't work, but otherwise it's a hell of a lot better than an eyewitness."

I liked Roger. He was objective. A week before we could have been friends.

I was attached to the machine by my arms and one hand, my jugular, left armpit, and temple. They took my blood pressure beforehand and then attached a thimblelike cap to my left index finger to keep track of my heart.

They started with simple questions about my name, my marital status, my job. They asked me did I love my wife and I said no. They asked did I want to hurt her and I said no. They asked me if I had ever committed a crime and I said, not to my knowledge.

We went through preparatory questions like these for twenty minutes by the digital clock that sat on a table to my right.

After that the serious questions started.

"Did you kill Sean Messier?"

"No."

"Did you strike him with a crowbar?"

"No."

"Do you know Barbara Knowland?"

"Yes."

"Where did you meet her?"

"I don't know."

"You don't remember?"

"That's right."

"How long ago did you meet her?"

"Probably more than twenty years ago, back in Colorado."

"Have you ever been to Sean Messier's house with her?"

"Not to my knowledge. You see, I only have one fleeting memory of her lying on a sofa. It seems real enough, but that's all I can remember."

When the lie detector test was over, Meeks came back at me. He asked me about Harvard Rollins.

"Why does he have such a hard-on for you in this thing?" Meeks asked.

"He's having an affair with my wife."

"Did you go to Knowland's hotel room?"

"Yes."

"Why?"

"To ask her to explain what was happening. She claims that I killed someone and I have absolutely no knowledge of that."

"What did she tell you?"

I repeated what she said word for word.

When I was through, the room went silent. For long moments we just sat there, eleven men and women communing with some external force.

"Is that all you need, Mr. Meeks?" Leonard Gideon asked at last.

"I'd like to know how to keep in touch with your client, Mr. Gideon."

"You have my card."

"He lives with you?"

The lawyer smiled and stood up.

"I could still have Mr. Dibbuk arrested as a material witness," Meeks exclaimed.

"At the Brown Palace maybe," Gideon said. "But the Plaza is in New York state and you couldn't arrest a cockroach here."

I took all my money out of the various accounts I owned and gave most of it to Cass.

"Put it someplace safe," I said to him.

I quit my job and moved permanently into Svetlana's studio. She seemed very happy to have me there. She got a job at a bookstore and told me to take at least six months off.

"You need to rest," Svetlana told me. "Take it easy for a while and then, later on, you can do something else and I will finish my school."

We made love every night, and in the morning I'd sit in my chair trying to remember Star and what we had done, or not, that long ago day.

I was still in therapy too. I paid Dr. Shriver in cash and he gave me a discount.

Six weeks after my deposition Leonard Gideon called me.

"They decided that there wasn't enough of a case to prosecute," he told me. "But if I were you, I wouldn't plan any ski vacations in Aspen anytime soon."

"How much do I owe you, Mr. Gideon?"

"I was happy to help a friend, Ben," he said.

I knew that I was not the friend he was helping but I was grateful anyway.

★   ★   ★

175

Svetlana got pregnant and Mona moved in with, then broke up with, Harvard Yard. Since I was without a job, our lawyer told us that I could ask for alimony but I demurred.

Seela hates me now. Dr. Shriver found her a therapist who uncovered all the damage I had done to her. She sees the divorce as me abandoning her—that, and she can't stand the idea of me with a woman as young as Svetlana.

They arrested Barbara Knowland after questioning her sister about the car they junked back in the late seventies. In her attempt to save herself from me, she put herself on trial. It seems that when her sister was deposed, she said things about the murder that were never in the news.

I get together with Cass on Thursday evenings at Joey's Steak House. We never talk about anything important or emotional. I still don't know a thing about sports, and talking about sex is definitely a no-no. But we seem to have a good time anyway.

I had been slipping back into my old ways with Svetlana. The numbness and the distance were always threatening to descend. And then one day I saw a news clip online as I was looking around for a new job.

AUTHOR BARBARA KNOWLAND FOUND GUILTY OF
1979 MURDER AND CRIMINAL NEGLIGENCE,
SENTENCED TO LIFE PLUS 30 YEARS

At the trial Barbara maintained that I had been the killer. The defense and the prosecution wanted me to testify but I kept telling them that I had no knowledge of the murder, the man, or even of Star herself. Whatever she thought had nothing at all to do with me.

I never went to Colorado or participated with either side of the trial.

That night was Lana's last night of work. I told her that I could cover the rent until she delivered and after that I'd get a job.

I felt secure in the presence of the Russian's ferocious love. I didn't understand it and I couldn't share its intensity most of the time. But its power was like a great beating heart that protected me.

After she'd fallen asleep, I dozed off sitting there next to her. I had a dream.

∾

I was with Barbara Knowland on a blue couch that stood upon a white shag carpet. We were having quite vigorous sex. I remembered, somewhere outside of the dream, that when I was drunk or high I could really enjoy sex. Barbara was looking up into my eyes, her whole body shuddering every time I slammed into her. She screamed but not in pain or pleasure. And then someone grabbed my shoulder and pulled me to my feet.

It was a big guy wearing a greenish leather jacket and a cowboy hat, the stranger from my medieval dream.

He said something in the dream that wasn't clear but I knew that he wanted me to go outside with him.

The next thing I knew, we were out next to a barn near a woodpile. I was naked, standing in the mud, and he was fully dressed. The rain was coming down.

"Let me tell you what I'm gonna do, son," the white man said to me in a frighteningly calm voice. I was drunk and nude—as vulnerable as you could get.

"I'm gonna beat you to the ground and then I'm gonna shove your head in with one'a them there logs." He hit me then, hard. I went down and he turned to get the log to kill me with. I jumped to my feet and leaped on his back. He twisted around and hit me twice. I fell again. He turned again. I struggled up and got him in a bear hug from behind. I was begging him not to kill me.

"You should'a thought about that before you broke my window," he said.

"I'll pay for it," I cried.

"You sure will," he promised.

He twisted around, breaking my grip, and hit me three times. I tried to hit him back but he had pugilist training. He made it to the woodpile that time and hefted a log that had to weigh twenty pounds. I ran at him and he threw the log at me. It hit me with a glancing blow to the head. I went down but the fear of death kept me from going unconscious.

There was a length of steel pipe next to me. The cowboy had turned back to the woodpile. And then, for one brief moment in eternity, I became the soul of human perfection. I grabbed the pipe and willed myself to a standing position. I staggered forward as he was hefting an even larger log. As he turned, I swung and the pipe landed perfectly on his right temple. I remembered the feel and the sound of bone crunching. And then I remembered nothing until it was night and I was coming awake in the muddy yard.

I didn't see his body, didn't really remember it. I went to the house and found my clothes. The pipe was still in my hand. I dressed, took the pipe to my car, and drove for hours. Somewhere along the way I threw the pipe down an embankment. A little after that I parked and drank from the last whiskey bottle in my trunk.

By morning all I had to remember the past day was a cut on my scalp along with a few bruises, nothing out of the ordinary. There had been a woman and a fight, but by the time I was back home, those memories might as well have been dreams.

~

The sleeping vision woke me up. It was just after three in the morning and Svetlana was asleep. I wondered if I should call Winston Meeks. Star was innocent. She hadn't killed anyone. But she did steal his money and his car. She had left me to shift for myself in the company of Sean Messier's corpse. And she had tried to build a case against me with the Colorado D.A. and in *Diablerie*.

I looked down at my young girlfriend and a feeling of love rushed through me. I kissed her temple and she smiled. It occurred to me that the emotion I was feeling went far beyond Svetlana. It had little or nothing to do with Star Knowland's self-demolition or the lucky break I got with the Colorado courts. There was an exhilaration in the dream I had. I was the killer. I had taken Sean Messier's life. It wasn't murder. It was most certainly self-defense, though I could have never proven that. But I didn't need proof.

My whole life I had felt naked and defenseless, under the authority of a force much greater than me. When Messier dragged me out into the yard and explained to me how he was going to end my life, I felt that this had been the place I'd been coming to since I was a child. I gave up, accepted death, and then went through the motions of trying to survive.

The memory of my victory gave me a feeling of elation, but not only that: The emptiness in my heart was suddenly filled. I was a whole man lying there next to that Russian child. I was a complete person—flawed, guilty, craven to a degree, but still these things and my victory made me whole.

I got up out of bed and sat in my favorite maple chair, naked. I was leaning forward with my elbows on my knees and my fingertips all touching. The dream I had was like a vision for Joan of Arc or some other religious zealot. It was like a deity touching my mind, awakening my imperfect humanity.

The path I'd traveled was strewn with victims: my wife and daughter, Sean Messier, Grant Timmons, and Star Knowland, even my mother, who stood in the shadows while my father beat me with love in his heart. My brother, I felt, was my victim too.

I thought back over my many crimes and misdemeanors. But I felt no remorse, only a giddy happiness. I'd been waiting for this moment with no hope of ever achieving it. I hadn't even known that I was my own hero, that I stood up to my death. And though I approached this test begging and whimpering, I still won.

These thoughts were part of a long train of ideas that passed through my mind that late evening. The sun began to rise and Svetlana reached out in her sleep. When she didn't find me there, she sat up.

"Ben?"

"Don't ever call me 'Benny' okay, honey?"

She blinked at me and nodded.

"What are you doing?" she asked.

"Thinking that maybe we should stop smoking," I said. "It's really not good for the baby, you know."

A NOTE ON THE AUTHOR

Walter Mosley is the best-selling author of more than twenty-eight critically acclaimed books; his work has been translated into twenty-one languages. His books include two popular mystery series, the Easy Rawlins series (beginning with *Devil in a Blue Dress*, which was adapted into a successful 1995 film starring Denzel Washington) and the Fearless Jones series, as well as literary fiction, science fiction, political monographs, and a young adult novel. His short fiction has been widely published, and his nonfiction has been published in the *New York Times Magazine* and the *Nation*, among other magazines. He was an editor and contributor to the book *Black Genius* and was guest editor for *The Best American Short Stories 2003*. He is the winner of numerous awards, including an O. Henry Award, a Grammy Award (for his liner notes to Richard Pryor's box set), and the PEN American Center's Lifetime Achievement Award. Walter Mosley was born and raised in Los Angeles and now lives in New York City.

A NOTE ON THE TYPE

The text of this book is set in Bembo. This type was first used in 1495 by the Venetian printer Aldus Manutius for Cardinal Bembo's *De Aetna*, and was cut for Manutius by Francesco Griffo. It was one of the types used by Claude Garamond (1480–1561) as a model for his Romain de L'Université, and so it was the forerunner of what became standard European type for the following two centuries. Its modern form follows the original types and was designed for Monotype in 1929.